MW01153111

Forever Lo

Devil's Knights MC

Book Nine

Wall Street Journal & USA Today Bestselling Author
Winter Travers

For questions or comments about this book, please
contact the author at winter@wintertravers.com

Black Belt Knockout

Nitro Crew Series
Burndown
Holeshot
Redlight
Shutdown

Sweet Love Novellas
Sweet Burn
Five Alarm Donuts

Stand Alone Novellas
Kissing the Bad Boy
Daddin' Ain't Easy
Silas: A Scrooged Christmas
Wanting More
Mama Didn't Raise No Fool
Room 19: The Last Resort Motel

Table of Contents

Chapter One

Meg

"I'm wearing yellow."

"Meg."

I looked up from my bowl of cereal. "Yes?"

Lo leaned against the kitchen counter and crossed his arms over his chest. "You're kidding."

I wasn't. Not in the least. "No."

"I don't think I have ever seen you in yellow and suddenly you're going to wear a yellow dress to your only son's wedding?" He scoffed and reached for a coffee cup. "You're going to end up wearing black."

I rolled my eyes and slurped back some milk in my bowl. "I can't do that, Lo." I wiped my mouth with the back of my hand. "If I wear black everyone is going to think I don't approve of Harlyn and that's not true."

"No, everyone is going to be fine with you wearing black because they know that you only wear black. If you show up to Remy's wedding wearing a yellow dress, everyone is going to think you're either having some mid-life crisis or that you have a brain tumor that is messing with your brain."

I rolled my eyes. "Really, Lo? Those are the only reasons why people would think I'm wearing yellow? Mid-life crisis or tumor?" I slurped the last of my milk and set the bowl down with a clatter. "You really have no faith in me."

"Well, seeing as it's Saturday and Remy is getting married a week from today, yeah, I don't have much faith in you seeing as you haven't even bought a dress for the wedding yet. You get a yellow dress, and you're going to look like a fucking canary."

I scrunched up my nose. "I have plenty of time and you sound like you don't think I'll look good in a yellow dress."

Lo pushed off the counter and pulled me up from my chair. He wrapped me up in his arms and I tipped my head back to look at him. "Never said you wouldn't look good. Said you would look like a fucking canary."

I quirked an eyebrow. "So you're into fucking canaries now?"

"We really going to get into this?" he growled.

I didn't really want to, but getting Lo riled up was kind of fun. "I'm just going off what you said."

His nostrils flared. "Babe, I'm into you, and if you want to dress up like a fucking canary, then go for it. Just don't come crying to me after you see the wedding pictures and you stick out like a sore thumb."

The urge to argue with him was strong, but I knew that everything he said was right. The idea of a yellow dress seemed fun and different in theory, but I knew I would end up regretting it. "Yellow is on the top of my list, but maybe I'll check out some other colors too."

"Like black," he replied flatly.

I pinched his nipple through his thin, black shirt. And twisted.

"Hey, hey, woman!" He knocked my hand away and placed his hand over his now twisted nipple. "Don't damage the goods."

I rolled my eyes and pushed him away. "I need to be at Cyn's in fifteen minutes."

"That means no quickie before you leave?"

I wagged my finger in his face. "You don't get to call me a canary and then think we're going to have sex." I grabbed my purse hooked over the chair. "Besides, you should have woken up earlier if you wanted that."

Lo scoffed. "Normally you wake me up with the smell of breakfast cooking, but you had cereal today. That ain't gonna wake me up."

"Forty-five years old and he expects me to wake him every morning." I rolled my eyes and dug around in my purse for my truck keys. "What are you doing today?" I spotted my keys and pulled them out.

"Gotta clean up the clubhouse before the reception next weekend and then maybe work on the bike."

"Work on the bike? What's wrong with it?"

Lo grabbed his coffee and leaned against the counter. "Putting a new exhaust on it. Got it in last week and I finally have time to work on it."

"What's wrong with the exhaust you have on it?"

He shrugged. "Nothing."

I closed one eye and pursed my lips. "You lost me on why you would order a new one then."

"Cause this one is gonna shake the neighbors windows."

Good lord. "I'm sure Larry will appreciate that."

"Fuck Larry. You would think after living here for almost ten years the guy would warm up to me a bit but nada."

"You really think Larry is going to come over and shoot the shit with you in the driveway while you wax your bike every Saturday?" Lo was crazy if he thought Larry was going to be buddies with him. I was just glad Larry kept to himself and didn't give us shit for the bikes and people coming and going from the house all the time.

"No."

"Then what the hell, Lo?"

He shrugged his shoulders. "I thought about it for a second and decided I was good with the guy not talking to me."

"And you tell me I'm the crazy one." I rolled my eyes and leaned up on my tip toes. "I'll be back later." I pressed a kiss to his cheek.

He grabbed me around the waist. "That kiss ain't gonna do it for me, babe." He pressed his lips to mine, and I slipped right into the Lo Daze. Though, I had to say I basically lived there permanently the past ten years. "Behave. I don't want any phone calls needing me to bail you out."

"One time that happened and you just won't let me live it down."

His hands squeezed my waist. "That one time got us banned from the furniture store for life."

"Pfft. I still say that was all Ethel's fault." You break one bed in the furniture store and bam, banned for life. "He was an angry nugget of a man, anyway."

"That was not my mother's fault at all. I'll have to let her know when I see her that you are still trying to blame that on her." Lo pulled me close and buried his face in my neck.

"You're such a mama's boy," I grumbled.

"Gotta love her while she's still here with us."

Ethel had another cancer scare six months ago, and I knew it had changed Lo. He realized he wasn't going to have his mom around forever. I closed my eyes and enjoyed the feel of being in this loving man's arms. "We do have a plate of her's that you could drop off to her on the way to the shop."

"Guess I could drop it to her," he whispered.

"Mama's boy."

He playful pushed me out his arms. "I'm gonna have to say you have your own mama's boy due in town in a couple of days."

I shook my finger at him. "You're damn straight, I have my own mama's boy. Though he could stand to call me a bit more."

Lo followed me to the front door and held it open for me. "I tell him all the time to call you, babe. I think he's afraid of the crazy stories you're gonna tell him."

I blew a raspberry. "He should be used to it by now. The boy has known my craziness for the past twenty-seven years." I pressed another quick kiss to Lo's lips. "Now I got to drive fast to get to Cyn's on time. You're too distracting." I pushed out the screen door and glared at Lo over my shoulder. "Have fun playing with your exhaust today."

Lo shook his head and rolled his eyes.

Larry was walking past the house with his tiny fluff ball of a dog and of course heard me. "Uh, hey there, Larry."

I could hear Lo's boisterous laugh from inside the house.

"Asshole," I hiss through the screen door.

It was only ten o'clock, and I had already made a fool of myself.

Just another day living the life.

*

Chapter Two

Lo

"Jesus Christ!" I stumbled backward out the door and slammed it shut before I fell back on my ass.

"Logan Birch! Why in the hell are you walking into my house without knocking?"

I scrubbed my hand down my face and asked myself the same question. I was catapulted back to a young child walking in on their parents doing the nasty. Full body shiver.

"Hush, woman," Gravel grumbled through the closed door.

"Who in the hell does that in the middle of the day with the door unlocked?" I hollered.

The front door swung open and Gravel glared down at me. Shirtless. Top button of his jeans unbuttoned. "We ain't fucking dead, son. Figured everyone who would stop by would be at work or out doing shit."

"Here." I shielded my arm over my eyes and held out the plate that belonged to Mom. "Just take this." I was going to need to go to the clubhouse and rinse my eyes out with bleach.

"You think you would have learned from the last time you did this." Mom's voice joined Gravel's but I didn't want to look. God only knew if she managed to get all of her clothes back on. "Knock on the damn door, Logan."

Mom was mad. She really only called me Logan when she was pissed off or trying to be serious. "Lock the damn door," I countered.

"You think we planned this?" Gravel asked. "One thing lead to another and before I knew it I had your mother bent over-."

"Stop!" I thundered. I had seen the visual, I didn't need the play-by-play of how it went down. I scrambled to my feet and turned my back to Gravel and mom. "I, uh, I'll see you guys at the wedding." Lord knows if I was going to be able to make eye contact with either of them. "Lock your damn door." I stomped down the steps and over to my bike.

Mom cackled like a mad woman and Gravel's low rumble laugh followed me till I peeled out of the driveway.

I couldn't hear them laughing anymore, but god knew I was forever going to be haunted with the image of my mom bent over the couch and begging Gravel to go harder.

Vomit rose up my throat, and I didn't make it to the clubhouse before emptying my stomach on the side of the road.

Twice.

*

Chapter Three

Meg

"That's the one."

"Lord have mercy, you look good."

I did. I looked amazing. "I'm not getting this one."

Cyn's jaw dropped and the bubble Gwen was blowing popped loudly. "Come again, girlfriend?" Gwen gasped.

"Unzip me, now." I turned my back to Cyn. "Did you not hear what I said earlier. I cannot buy a black dress. Get it off me, now." This was not going to happen. "Do you think they have it in yellow? Maybe orange." I glanced over my shoulder at Cyn who hadn't budged from the chair she was sitting in.

"Uh, girl. You cannot rock yellow or orange." Gwen shook her head. "At least not in a mother of the bride dress. We could do some funky highlights in your hair if you want though."

"Cyn," I hissed. "Snap out of it and get me out of this dress. Pronto."

Cyn shook her head. "Only if you promise to me that you are not going to buy a yellow or orange dress. You are not a bright color person, chick. Why don't you try plum or dark blue?"

I turned to the mirror to the side. I ran my hands down the satin fabric and sighed. "I'm not doing blue cause that's your thing. I'll match Rigid's hair and that will just be awkward."

"How's it going in here?" Peg, the salesclerk slipped into the dressing room with a platter and champagne glasses.

Yes, booze will make this better. I grabbed a glass from her and chugged it down in three gulps. I set the empty glass on the platter and grabbed another. "I'm gonna need this dress in purple, Peg."

Peg blinked at the empty champagne glass. I don't think she was used to customers like Cyn, Gwen, and I. "I, ah, let me look at the tag." She offered the tray of glasses to Cyn and Gwen then set it on the small table next to the seatette they were sitting on. She fumbled with the tag and cleared her throat. "Uh, that dress comes in the black you have on, or white."

"Oh hell no!" Cyn jumped up and yanked the zipper down. "If you're not going to get the black, then you sure as hell aren't going to get the white." She grabbed my glass from me and set it on the table.

"Well, duh," I grumbled. Black would make me look like I didn't approve of Harlyn and the white would make it look like I was trying to upstage her.

"Cover the girly bits and let's go look at the racks. There has to be something out there that is perfect." Gwen grabbed my shirt and tossed it at me.

I smirked and pulled the shirt over my head. The dress pooled at my feet and I stepped out of it. "You mean I can't go out there in my underwear?"

Peg choked and lightly patted her chest. "Uh, that would not be the best idea." Cyn snatched my pants off the floor and handed them to me. "Put your damn clothes on, woman. You and I both know you wouldn't step foot out of here without being clothed."

"Clothed?" Gwen snickered.

"How is she tipsy after only having one glass of champagne?" I asked. I tugged my pants on and grabbed my glass of champagne. "And for the record, we always need to shop at places that offer booze."

Gwen lead the way out of the dressing room and over to the four racks of mother of the bride dresses. "There has to be a dress in here that is going to be the one."

I nodded my head. "Yup. There has to be."

Cyn grabbed the hem of a lime green dress. "But it's not this one."

Agreed. "I think first we need to just look at color. Pick out the colors that will work and then whittle them down by style."

Gwen tipped her glass to me. "I think shopping and drinking booze works for you. That was a very smart idea."

I knocked the green dress from Cyn's hand. "Thank you. Now, let's get to work, ladies, and prove Lo wrong."

"And what was it again that we're proving him wrong about?"

I reached to grab Gwen's glass from her but she sidestepped out of my grasp. "You are not taking my mama juice right now. I have a six and four-year-old at home and I can't remember the last time I was free for a whole afternoon."

Cyn clinked her glass against Gwen's. "A-fucking-men to that, sister. Micha just turned eleven and I swear to god it's like he's eighteen." Cyn shook her head. "You would think it would be enough for him to be able to do whatever he wants with his hair, but now he's begging Rigid to get his ear pierced and a tattoo."

I clicked my tongue. "Go with the earring but tell him auntie Meg says he has to wait on the tattoo. At least sixteen."

"Meg," Cyn gasped. "His ass is waiting until he is eighteen to get either."

Gwen chuckled. "I find it hilarious that you let the kid dye his hair any color he wants but you're freaking out over an earring."

Cyn rolled her eyes. "Because I can cut his hair off and it'll grow back. You think I can cut his ear off and it'll grow back?"

Gwen and I looked at each other. "Uh, can't you just take the earring out? I mean, there will be a tiny hole there, but I think cutting his ear off would be a bit drastic." Thank god Micha had me around or he would be Picasso walking around.

"It's about the principle," Cyn huffed.

"You're married to a man with blue hair, covered in tattoos, and from the stories you've told, pierced in," I cleared my throat, "places the eyes can't see."

"Like we are ones to talk," Gwen laughed. "I think we all married men like that."

22

We looked from one to the other. "A-fucking-men to that!" we cheered in unison.

"Now, let's find me a dress so we can get to the hibachi place." I drained my glass and tucked it under my arm. Good food was our end game. "I want black, but not black."

"Sounds easy enough," Cyn laughed.

Twenty minutes later we were back in the dressing room with a fresh bottle of champagne and fifteen dresses.

"Those five are out right off the bat." I tugged my shirt over my head. "Let's just agree then these arms need sleeves, yeah?" I didn't feel like getting out on the dance floor at the wedding and having my arm fat waving at everyone. I lifted my arm and watched my loose chicken wings flap. "Ridiculous," I grumbled.

Cyn grabbed the five sleeveless dresses and hung them on the opposite wall. "So, this will be the reject wall."

Gwen grabbed a deep yellow dress. "Who in the hell grabbed this one? I thought we decided that yellow was not the color for Meg?"

Cyn grabbed it and hung it on the reject wall. "I thought we could give it a whirl, seeing as it wasn't a bright ass yellow. I didn't know we hated every shade of yellow."

Gwen and Cyn argue back and forth about the color yellow while Peg helped me into my first dress.

"Pfft, blah, urgh, gah," I sputtered. Peg zipped the dress up in the back and I batted down the large ruffle around my shoulders. "What in the hell is this?"

Peg turned me toward the mirror and Cyn and Gwen stopped bickering. "This is a mermaid off the shoulder with a ruffle. The color is regency."

"Oh, uh," Cyn muttered.

Gwen searched for her words. "The, well, uh, color is nice."

"It is very mermaid esque," I muttered.

"It's awful!" Cyn blurted. "You look like a damn clown with the puffy collar around your shoulders."

"Accurate," Gwen agreed.

"So, we'll take the clown mermaid dresses out and put them on the reject wall." Peg picked through the dresses and placed two on the opposite wall along with the first offending dress.

The next six dresses went by quickly with no real winners.

"This one has to work." Cyn fingered the lacy sleeve.

"At least it's a pretty purple." Gwen grabbed the dress from the hook and slid it off the hanger.

"This is brand new. I actually haven't seen it on anyone yet." Peg grabbed the dress from Gwen and helped me into it.

It fit snugly across my bodice, the lace sleeves glided up my arms and Peg zipped up the back.

"Holy. Shit," Cyn gasped.

"Why in the hell didn't we try this one first? It would have saved us half an hour and a bottle of champagne." Gwen circled around me with her hand covering her mouth.

"A-line, chiffon and lace with a scoop neck. It's actually breathtaking on you." Peg fluffed out the bottom of the dress and I watched in amazement as it floated back around me.

"You're like a purple goddess." Cyn circled the opposite direction of Gwen. "Lo is going to blow his load when he sees you." Cyn and Gwen high fived and laughed.

"Uh, so that means this is the one?" Peg asked. She was once again a bit taken back by the open and crassness of our group.

I twirled around and knew I looked psychotic with the huge smile on my face, but I couldn't stop. "We have a winner, Peg. Wrap it up and point me in the direction of the hibachi place."

*

Chapter Four

Lo

"When Mal and I get married, you can bet your ass we are not going to do it at the clubhouse."

I kicked my feet out in front of me and popped open a beer. "You think you're too good to get married here?" I asked Turtle.

He shook his head and wiped his forehead with the back of his hand. "Not that at all. I just don't want to be the one to clean this fucking place and organize a million chairs."

"You even ask her to marry you yet?" Turtle had been seeing Mal for four years and he had a three-year-old with her. How he had managed to snag the new lawyer in town was beyond me, but they seemed very much in love.

A huge smile spread across Turtle's lips. "I was gonna do it Saturday night."

"At the wedding?"

He nodded his head. "She's been dropping hints about getting married for the past year and I've been acting like I don't hear her."

"But you do."

Turtle nodded his head. "I hear her, but I'm going to need your guys help."

Rigid walked into the clubhouse from the garage. "Help? How much more fucking help do we need? All the chairs are finally set up and that arch thing is in the garage. We just gotta haul it in here Friday after the rehearsal dinner."

"No, not the wedding." Turtle plopped down on the couch next to me. "I'm gonna ask Mal to marry me here, but I booked a room at a hotel two towns over and was hoping you and Meg would be able to watch Jonas overnight for us."

Rigid snickered and turned on the TV. "You are the only ones that don't have kids under the age of ten besides Slider and Fayth."

"They're headed out of town early Sunday morning. Something about Marco needing help with his new house." Turtle sighed. "I really hate to ask but I've made Mal wait long enough for me to ask her to marry her."

I clapped Turtle on the back. "Don't worry about it, brother. You know Meg loves Jonas."

Turtle sighed. "Thank you. I didn't want to ask, but I really didn't have another choice. I don't plan on doing it till later on in the night."

I nodded my head. "I'll have to tell her to lay off the wine coolers, but she'll be fine with it."

Rigid chuckled. "Good luck with that."

"Maybe I'll be the one taking care of Jonas after you leave." I didn't want to have to tell Meg she couldn't drink at her only son's wedding. "I think we all plan on staying at the clubhouse the night of the wedding anyway so we'll all be able to keep an eye on Jonas."

The bedrooms at the clubhouse rarely got used for more than storage these days. Most of the guys had houses or apartments and just used their rooms to store shit for the clubhouse in them.

"Speaking of which," Rigid cleared his throat. "Cyn and all the girls told me we better put clean sheets on the bed or none of them are going to stay here."

"We still plan on putting all the kids in one or two rooms?" I asked. With nine kids ranging from three to eleven, we had to have somewhere for them to sleep.

Rigid flipped through the channels on the TV. "Three sets of bunk beds will be here Wednesday and the mattresses for them will be here Thursday."

"Cutting it kind of fucking close, aren't you?" With all of us being in our mid-thirties and up you would think we would have our shit together a bit more.

"Figure as long as they get here before Saturday night we'll be good."

"Better fucking hope they get here before Saturday, or you'll be the one putting them together during the ceremony." I shook my head.

"Or have all the kids staying at your house." Turtle snickered.

"They'll be here," Rigid assured us.

They better be. I was fine having to watch the kids, but I drew the line to having them share my bed with me and Meg.

That had been a no kid zone for the past ten years, and there were no signs in that ever changing.

*

Chapter Five

Meg

"My shoes should be here today."

Cyn slowly raised her head. "What do you mean?"

"I mean my shoes should be delivered today." I cut off the end of the onion and started chopping it.

"Meg, the wedding is in three and a half days. You don't have shoes?"

I rolled my eyes and scoffed. "Of course I have shoes, Cyn." I dumped the diced onions into a bowl. "They're being delivered today."

Cyn blinked slowly. "Do you think procrastination this long is going to work out for you?" She slowly stirred the beans and grabbed her margarita glass.

It was Tuesday, and we had bumped our monthly Si Senor! Margaritas and Taco night to tonight because Remy and Harlyn didn't want to have it as their rehearsal dinner. I had started the meat yesterday and now Cyn and I were working on everything else.

"The shoes will be here. I checked the tracking this morning."

"Meg." Cyn's eyes connected with mine. "It's past five o'clock. The mail has ran and the UPS guy comes around ten thirty."

"Uh, come again?" And how the hell did Cyn know the times that UPS rolled through.

"Your shoes are not coming today."

"How do you know that? Also, how do you know what time UPS runs?"

She rolled her eyes. "Uh, hello. I order shit and don't want Rigid to know because he tells me I'm spending all the money on senseless shit."

"Are you?" I had been to Cyn's house. She had some shit I wondered why she would even buy. "And I guess they're going to come tomorrow then."

"Who's side are you on, Meg? I can't help it that Morphe came out with a new pallet and then Too Faced came out with one right after it. It's completely out of my hands."

"Are you talking a different language right now?"

"Makeup, Meg. I'm talking about makeup."

I scrunched up my nose. "Girl, I get my eyeshadows and eyeliner from the Walgreens. Five ninety-nine for ten eyeshadows, you can't go wrong."

Cyn pointed the spoon she was stirring with at me. "Pigment, Meg. You're lacking pigment."

"I'm really worried about you." I set the knife down and folded my hands together. "I think we need to have an intervention."

"Who needs an intervention?" Lo walked in the back door with a case of beer in one hand and three plastic bags in the other.

"Cyn. She's blowing Rigid's retirement on makeup." I popped a piece of pepper in my mouth and smiled at Lo.

"I've heard. Rigid mumbles about pigment under his breath all the time." Lo set the bags on the table and brushed a kiss against my lips. "Guys will be here in half an hour."

Cyn huffed and turned back to the stove. "The hellion is in the backyard with Diamond. Micha was wondering when Uncle Lo was going to get here."

"What's he need?" Lo asked.

Cyn shook her head. "He's trying to rally people to take his side about getting his ear pierced."

"And?"

Cyn glared at Lo over her shoulder. "He is eleven years old, Lo. He doesn't need to start piercing things this early."

"Got my ear pierced when I was ten. I think I turned out just fine."

I brushed my fingers over Lo's crotch. "I think you just helped Cyn's argument that if he gets his ears pierced now, it's just going to lead to him piercing other things."

Cyn dropped the spoon in the beans. "Jesus, Meg! Did you really need to go there? I never in a million years ever want to think about that and Micha in the same thought."

"You don't want him to be like father like son?" Lo teased.

Cyn's cheeks heated and turned red. "You're both assholes, you know? He has no clue that Rigid has, well," her eyes darted to Lo's crotch, "that. And he will never know."

"Right," Lo drawled. He grabbed a beer and popped open the top. "I'll go talk to him and see if I can hold him off till he's sixteen."

"Or seventy," Cyn yelled at his retreating back.

"Girl," I laughed. "You are one big contradiction."

"Don't I know it," she mumbled.

Cyn kept stirring the beans while I chopped, diced, and prepped all the toppings and sides.

"You doing my job, woman?" Rigid walked through the front door and slid his sunglasses on top of his head.

"If you would have been here, I wouldn't have had to do it." Cyn took the pan off the heat and turned off the burner. "Micha is in the backyard with Lo."

"That kid is relentless." Rigid shook his head.

"That's all you," Cyn muttered.

"Hey," Rigid protested. "I'm in agreement with you on this, baby. He can wait until he's sixteen to get his ears pierced just like I did."

Cyn wiped her hands on the dish towel. "Well then maybe you should tell him that instead of magically disappearing every time he brings it up."

Rigid held up his hands. "All right, all right. I'm on it. Cool your jets." Rigid pulled out his phone. "I'll find some pictures of infected piercings and shit. That should deter him." Rigid typed on his phone and instantly cringed.

"Ears, Rigid. Nothing else."

Rigid looked up at Cyn. "This almost made me want to take my piercings out." He held up the phone, and I instantly ducked my head knowing he was about to show us something absolutely disgusting.

Cyn gagged and tossed the dish towel at Rigid. "You are an asshole."

Rigid walked out the back door chuckling under his breath.

"It was a dick, wasn't it?" I didn't want to see it, but I was curious about what it was.

"If you would call it that. The thing was green and pussy."

I clutched my hand to neck and closed my eyes. "Sweet Jesus. I didn't need a description."

"I should have had a girl I know for the rest of my life it's just going to be Rigid and Micha grossing me out."

I ripped open the bag of shredded lettuce and dumped it in a bowl. "I think we're all destined to that seeing as out of nine kids running around, only two are girls." Thank god Marley and Gwen were able to overcome the strong alpha gene and give us Luna and Greta.

Cyn raised her margarita glass toward me. "Amen to that, sister."

*

Lo

"What the hell is this?" Slide lifted a Mounds bar up. "I thought you said you had shit for s'mores."

Meg plopped down in my lap. "That's for island s'mores."

"What in the hell is an island s'more, woman? I want a s'more s'more. Graham, chocolate, marshmallow, graham." Slider motioned by stacking his hands on top of each other. "S'more."

The adults were spread out around the fire and the kids were running around playing tag and trying to catch fireflies. I was stuffed from dinner, but apparently Slider had room for a little dessert.

"There's peanut butter cups there too," Meg pointed out.

36

Slider threw down the Mounds bar and shook his head. "This is ridiculous. It's a sad day when a guy can't even get an OG s'more."

"I think this falls under first world problems," Fayth called. "There are kids starving in Africa and you're complaining about the wrong candy for your s'more."

Slider sat down in the chair next to her. "I don't really remember asking you."

Fayth flipped him off. "We're married. My opinion is the only one that matters."

Meg laughed and laid her head on my shoulder. "Should I tell him I have a few Hershey bars in the house?"

I pressed a finger to Meg's lips. "Shh. It's always good when Fayth puts him in his place."

"Isn't that every day?" Meg laughed.

"Yeah, but I don't always get to see it."

Meg cuddled into me and sighed. "How has this been our life for ten years?"

I held her close and looked around the fire pit. Kids were running around like crazy and the best friends I could ever have were surrounding me. "Guess we're just fucking lucky, babe."

"Ain't that the truth," she murmured. "You have everything ready for the wedding?"

The guys and I had been working on shit for the wedding for the past four days. It would have been only three days, but Gambler had brought the kids with him the other day and they had managed to knock over the archway for the ceremony. That was something Meg didn't know and wouldn't know until the day of the wedding.

"Clubhouse is fucking spotless, chairs are set up, and I pick up the tuxes on Friday."

Meg sighed and laid her hand on my chest. "I still can't believe Remy asked you to be one of his groomsmen."

I had been pretty fucking shocked too. "Pretty crazy. You raised a good kid, babe."

"I sure did. Now I just hope his dad doesn't make a scene at the wedding."

I wrapped my arms around her and held her close. "Well, we all know you know how to handle Hunter. A swift kick to the nuts will make him fall in line."

"If only that were true. He's bringing his new girlfriend and Remy told me she isn't like the other girls he has dated in the past."

"What's that mean?" I had only met one of the chicks Hunter dated and I was not impressed. He had definitely downgraded from Meg.

"He actually likes her." Meg's voice was quiet and I could tell she wasn't sure what to think or feel.

"Babe," I said softly.

"I'm being dumb, Lo. I know it. Just let me be dumb for a hot second while I think Remy is going to like her more than he likes me."

"Meg, you just said what you need to hear." I adjusted her in my lap and turned her toward me more. "He likes her, but he loves you. You're his mom and he's not going to find another mom at the age of twenty-eight."

"I know," she huffed. "I told you I was being dumb."

"Well, you can be dumb for the next ten minutes and then you better snap out of it."

She sighed heavily and closed her eyes. "You're too nice to me."

"Guess that's why I married you."

"So you can be nice to me every day?"

I pressed a kiss to the side of her head. "Damn straight, babe."

*

Chapter Six

Meg

I felt Lo roll out of bed and I moved to bury my face in his pillow.

"Get your ass up, woman. It's rehearsal day."

I groaned and held up my middle finger to Lo. "No. You kept me up too late last night."

"Pretty sure I tried to get you to come to bed three times last night."

I lifted my head and rolled over onto my back. "Remy came home. With his fiancée. Can you really blame me for wanting to stay up for a bit?"

Lo lifted one eyebrow. "You came to bed at two. I'm pretty sure that's more than staying up a little."

"Do you have a point, Mr. Birch?"

Lo pulled his shirt over his head and tossed it in the clothes hamper. He dropped the sweatpants he had on and his dick stood at attention. He looked down at his dick and smirked. "There's only one point here right now and I think it needs your attention."

I licked my lips and raised up on my elbows. "Then you better come back to bed."

"Was thinking of taking a shower."

I shook my head. "As amazing as that sounds, I'm pretty sure Remy and Harlyn wouldn't appreciate being woken up on the count of us having sex."

Lo scowled. "Damn. Been so long that Remy has been in his room that I forgot that he's right next to the shower."

I nodded my head and bite my lip. "Yup. But that doesn't mean we can't have a little fun in here."

Lo planted a knee on the bed. "Put some music on."

I rolled my eyes and grabbed my phone. "Worried?" I scrolled through my downloaded songs and picked the latest Lee Brice song.

"Not worried, just wanting to cover all of my bases to make sure Remy and Harlyn don't hear us." Lo crawled up the bed and grabbed my phone. "Never heard this song before." He tossed my phone on the nightstand and looked down at me.

I constantly had music playing around the house and the office at work. This was a new song, but it wasn't the first time I had listened to it. "You should open your ears. I've been playing it constantly for the past week."

Lo covered my body with his. "I tend to be distracted when I'm around you and only pay attention to you. Music and everything else is secondary."

I circled my arms around my neck. "You sure are a sweet talker, Lo."

A grin spread across his lips. "Just telling you like it is. Fell in love with you ten years ago, babe, and it hasn't changed a day since. But if you would have put on some AC/DC or Metallica, I totally would have known the song."

"So predictable," I muttered.

He pressed a kiss to my lips and tugged the blanket down my body. "And that's how you like it."

"I guess that makes me predictable, too."

He trailed kisses across my face and down my neck. "Only predictable thing about you, babe, is I know you'll always love me. Everything else is a Crapshoot with you."

"I can't deny that," I whispered. Keeping Lo on his toes was a full-time job. I didn't want him to get bored and find a younger and more fun version of me.

His hands traveled down my side and grabbed the hem of my shirt. He tugged it over my head and tossed it on the floor. "I wouldn't let you out of this bed if you denied it."

"Hmm, never leaving this bed sounds tempting. Were you trying to threaten me?" If I could get away with spending the rest of my life in bed with Lo, I would totally do it.

"Not much of a threat when I know the idea turns you on."

I ran my hands up and down his back. "You breathing turns me on, Lo."

He kissed me.

Hard.

Passionately.

Fully.

Lo's tongue slid into my mouth and my world exploded.

I couldn't get enough. I was never going to get enough of Logan Birch. President of the Devil's Knights MC and the only man in this world who could make me melt with one glance.

"Spread your legs, babe." His hand covered my mound, and I spread my legs wide.

"Permission to come aboard, captain."

"Fucking nut," Lo muttered.

"But I'm your nut," I whispered.

Lo's fingers felt like heaven between my legs. Stroking, flicking, and gliding over my clit.

"Lo, please," I gasped.

"You know the drill, babe. First you come all over my fingers, and then you get my dick." He pressed lazy kisses over my chest and sucked my nipple into his mouth.

My hips bucked up into his hand and my eyes slammed shut.

The combination of Lo's hand and mouth was something that always drove me crazy.

Lo drove me crazy.

My orgasm crashed over me. My pussy drenched and ready for Lo.

In one swift movement Lo's hand left my pussy. He grabbed my hips and flipped me over. I got up on all fours and moaned when I felt him behind me. "My favorite," I mumbled. Any sex with Lo was good sex, but this, this was the best. Feeling him behind me. Driving into me. Lord above, it was amazing.

Lo gathered my hair in his hand and tugged my head back. "Tell me."

"I want you, Lo."

"More," he growled.

"I need you." Almost every day Lo needed to hear that I needed him.

Every day I told him. Most of the time it was when he was buried deep inside me and my body ached for him.

I reared back into him, his dick buried to the hilt and a low moan escaped his lips. "Ten years. Ten years and I still can't get enough of you."

Lo pounded inside me. Driving into me with each thrust.

"Oh my god," I panted. His hand in my hair tugged and my head arched back. "Lo," I gasped.

"Take it, babe. Fucking take it."

I took it. I had no choice when it came to Lo. I would forever take whatever he wanted to give me and love it.

With each of my gasps, Lo moaned, and I panted through my release.

Lo growled, released my hair, and both of his hands gripped my hips. He pounded into me, my pussy milking his cock each time he pulled out and then drove back in.

There was nothing but Lo and I.

Nothing but me and the man of my dreams.

What a way to wake up every morning.

*

Chapter Seven

Meg

"Babe."

I blinked rapidly.

"Meg. We need to go."

I fanned my face and prayed for my mascara to dry lightning fast. "Hold your horses. I'm almost ready."

"You planned this damn rehearsal dinner, and we're going to be late to it." Lo leaned against the bathroom door.

My eyes traveled over him, and I said a silent thank you to Ethel for creating such a fine man. "We're not going to be late. I just need to find my shoes and we can go." And also finish my eyes and find a lip gloss that wasn't gloopy.

"Really?" he chuckled. "Shoes is all you need?"

I was also standing in front of the bathroom mirror in my underwear. "And my dress." Small detail.

"I'll let Remy know we're going to be late." He pulled his phone out and typed out a message.

Lo's phone dinged almost instantly. He chuckled and shook his head.

"What did he say?" I swiped on some smoky eyeshadow then dabbed some purple to the inside corner of each eye.

"Typical."

I laughed and finished up my eyes. "He lived with me for eighteen years. He should know how I roll."

A knock sounded at the door and Lo moved to answer it. "What in the hell is Larry doing here?" he growled.

"Not a clue." I rifled through my messy makeup bag and grabbed a lip gloss.

I could hear Lo's low timber but couldn't make out what he was saying. I finished up my makeup and flipped off the bathroom light. My dress was draped over the living room couch which happened to be right where Lo was talking to Larry.

Lo mumbled his thanks and finally shut the front door.

I dashed into the living room and grabbed the white dress with large black polka dots all over it. "What did Larry want?"

Lo turned from the door and held a rectangle box in his hands. "He said this was delivered to his house Tuesday."

My eyes lit up at the sight of the box. "My shoes!"

Lo scowled. "Woman. You have plenty of shoes. What in the hell are you ordering more for?"

I dropped my dress and snatched the box out of his hand. "These are wedding shoes, Lo. I can't wear just any shoes from my closet for my only son's wedding." I walked into the kitchen and grabbed the scissors out of the drawer. I ripped open the box and held my breath. My jaw dropped at the sight of the silver 2 inch strappy heels. "They're gorgeous."

"Babe."

I looked up at Lo. "What?"

"You're standing in the kitchen with a shoe in your hand and no clothes on. Either you need to get dressed or I'm gonna fuck you on the kitchen counter."

"We literally had sex a half an hour ago." Lo had come home exactly when I had gotten out of the shower. He figured it was a perfect time to fuck me since I was naked. I didn't argue with his thinking. "Which, may I point out, is part of the reason why I'm running behind on being ready."

Lo growled and took a step toward me. "You got two minutes to get that dress on, or you're going to miss the rehearsal dinner."

"Okay, okay," I grumbled. I dropped the shoe and box on the kitchen counter and scrambled to grab my dress. "It's sexy when you go all caveman on me, but honestly tonight is not the night for that." I held the dress in front of me and stepped into it. "You think you can control yourself long enough to zip me up and not rip my dress off?" I pulled the dress up, threaded my arms through the sleeves and turned my back to Lo.

He slowly pulled up the zipper and leaned close. "Four hours," he whispered.

"What?"

"You've got four hours of me controlling myself and then you're mine." He pressed a kiss to the sensitive skin behind my ear. A shiver ran up my body and leaned back into him.

"Is that a promise?"

"You know it is, babe."

I twisted around and wrapped my arms around his neck. "Then I better get my shoes on so we can get the hell out of here."

He chuckled low and pressed a kiss to my lips. "Hop to it, babe. Times running."

*

Chapter Eight

Lo

"How did you manage to finally get her out the door?"

I glanced at Remy. "I have my ways with your mom."

Remy cringed. "I shouldn't have asked."

I watched Meg from across the room as she threw her head back and laughed at something Harlyn had said. "You ready for tomorrow?"

Remy nodded his head. "Been ready since the day I asked Harlyn to marry me." He ran his finger around the collar of his shirt. "Asking her was more terrifying than this. Hell, getting Roc to agree to let me marry his daughter had been hell."

"But he agreed."

Remy nodded his head. "Sure fucking did. Though it was agreed upon that if I hurt Harlyn he can run me over with the race car a few times."

"So, you'll live but just a little worse for wear," I chuckled.

"More than likely dead. I've seen what one of those cars can do to a squirrel. Ain't no way that thing will run over me without ripping all of my skin off." Remy shook his head. "Low ground clearance."

"What in the hell are you talking about?" Jay, Remy's friend and best man, walked up with a heaping plate piled high.

"Roc," Remy replied simply.

Jay nodded his head. "Say no more."

Prior to eating we had ran through how tomorrow would go and then Meg had let everyone descend upon the huge buffet of food.

"You should have had Roc make his potato salad." Jay piled a forkful of corn into his mouth.

Remy shook his head. "This is mine and Harlyn's favorite foods, Jay, not yours."

"Dude," Jay mumbled around a mouthful. "That potato salad is everyone's favorite."

Remy rolled his eyes. "Just keep eating that mountain of food on your plate and stop thinking about Roc's potato salad."

"Who's talking about my potato salad?" Roc walked up with a beer in his hand.

Jay swallowed. "I was. You should have made a vat of it."

"A vat?" Roc growled. He turned to Remy. "How much has he had to drink?"

Remy shrugged. "Either none or not enough."

Roc nodded to me. "You cleaned this place up real nice, King."

I had told Roc he could call me Lo since he wasn't part of the club, but he insisted on calling me King. "Thanks."

"I still can't believe you grew up around a motorcycle club." Jay shook his head.

"I was sixteen when my mom started dating Lo, dumbass. I didn't grown up here."

"Major bummer."

Roc smacked Jay upside the head. "You're an idiot."

"Hey," Jay protested. "I'm slightly offended though I do resemble that remark."

Frankie came to stand next to Remy with her husband behind her. "Damn. Even off the track and out of the garage Roc is still smacking you."

Brooks leaned forward. "Were we the only ones who snuck into the garage and saw all the killer bikes and cars?"

Frankie elbowed him in the gut and Brooks face paled when he saw I was standing there. "Sorry Mr. King."

"Shut it," Frankie hissed.

I chuckled and nodded to the open door of the shop. "Not really sneaking when we leave the door open. Figured you guys would want to check out the garage." I knew what a gear head Remy was, and I figured his friends would be the same way.

Jay held his head above his hand and pointed to the garage. "Onward," he yelled.

Roc, Frankie, and Brooks followed and disappeared into the garage.

"You sure it's okay?" Remy asked.

I shrugged. "They probably know more about cars than I do. If they feel like tinkering with the Cutlass, I can't get the timing right on they are more than welcome to."

Remy laughed. "Leave it to Roc. He'll have it fixed by morning."

Remy took a step toward the garage and I snagged him by the arm. "One thing."

"Yeah?"

"Just…" I glanced at Meg. "Your mom was worried about you liking your dad's girlfriend. You know how she is." I knew there wasn't anything to worry about, but I wanted Remy to know that Meg was having a bit of a hard time with it.

"I know." Remy nodded his head toward his dad who was seated at one of the tables with his family. It was hard inviting the asshole into my clubhouse, but at the end of the day the guy was Remy's dad. "My dad is dealing with the same feelings since he found out I asked you to be one of my groomsmen."

"Hard pill for him to swallow?"

Remy nodded his head. "Yeah, but, you've been a part of my life for ten years. He gets it, but it's still hard for him."

"Maybe another ten years of me sticking around will help."

Remy chuckled. "I think he knows you're here to stay."

At least the guy was smart enough to realize that. "Your mom gets it too, but you know how she is. She's ruled by her emotions and forgets to take a step back sometimes before she reacts."

"She's got you, Lo." Remy clapped me on the shoulder. "I haven't worried about her for the past ten years." Remy smiled. "I'm not going to start again now." Remy headed in the direction of his friends and I sighed.

It was nice knowing I still had the kids approval after all of these years.

"There's my handsome husband." Meg was walking toward me with a huge grin on her lips.

I looked at the empty glass in her hand. "And there is my tipsy wife."

She tapped her nose. "Ding, ding, handsome. I am tipsy and extremely happy." She stood in front of me and rested her hand on my chest. "My son is marrying the perfect girl, I have my friends and family surrounding me."

I glanced over at Hunter and his family.

Meg waved her hand in their direction. "Well, not him. Though I swear his mother likes me more than she does him."

I chuckled and shook my head. "Only you could be divorced from a guy for fifteen years and still have his family like you."

She shrugged. "What can I say? I'm likeable."

I grabbed her around the waist and pulled her close. "What's say you and I sneak to my old room and I'll show you just how likeable you are."

"Has it been four hours already?" she gasped.

I pressed a kiss to her lips. "No, not even close. I guess I just can't seem to keep my hands off of you."

Meg looked around. "I suppose we could sneak off for a bit and no one will notice."

I glanced over at Hunter watching Meg and I. I moved my hand lower, over her ass, and gave her a squeeze. The asshole had never personally done anything to me, but you can bet your ass I would forever hate the douchebag for hurting Meg. Rubbing it in his face that I was the one who had ended up with the perfect woman was my small consolation to having to invite him into my clubhouse. "Think you can remember the way to my room?"

Meg laughed. She grabbed my hand and pulled me toward the hallway. "I think I can find the way."

*

Chapter Nine

Meg

"They don't fit."

"Say what?"

I hopped on one foot and tried to cram the shoe on my foot. "They don't fit," I grunted.

Cyn shook her head. "Now do you understand why I was so concerned about you buying shoes off of Amazon?"

I tried one last time but gave up when the circulation was cut off to my pinky toe. "I'm a size ten. I ordered a size ten. I don't understand how this is not a ten." I held up the offending shoe. "This is ridiculous."

"Probably cause you ordered them from a place overseas. You know those sizes run smaller than American sizes." Gwen finished pinning Paige's hair and took a step back. "I think I have an extra pair of shoes you can wear. I'm a ten and a half, but that's better than nothing, right?"

Holy crap. "Here?" I asked. Gwen was going to be lifesaver if she had a spare pair of shoes for me to wear.

The girls and I were tucked away in the back room of the clubhouse with Harlyn and Frankie. We had offered for Mave and Delaney to get dressed with us, but in the end it had been decided it would be best for Mave and Delaney to help the guys get ready.

Gwen nodded her head. "In my car. I'm notorious for wearing heels to work and halfway through my shift having to change into tennis shoes." Gwen dug through her purse and tossed her keys to Paige. "Run out to my car and see what shoes I have."

Paige rolled her eyes. "I bet you have at least ten pairs in there." She shook her head and stood up. "Any specific color you want?" Paige asked me.

"Silver or black?" Either would go with my dress. Honestly, I just needed shoes that weren't my tennis shoes.

Gwen started working on Harlyn's hair and I figured it was time for me to give her my gift.

I rummaged through my purse and pulled out a small box. I had searched high and low for the perfect gift. I had found it six months ago and then seen the price tag. I then searched high and low again and this time paid attention to prices.

"So, I really wanted to give you something that was mine, and before that my mom's, but to be honest, my mom and I really don't do that sort of thing."

Cyn snorted. "Girl, you have never said a truer thing."

I glared at Cyn. "Zip it, woman." She was interrupting my touching spiel I had planned. "As I was saying, I wanted to get you something special." I stepped toward Harlyn and held out the box to her. "Now, they're not worth millions, but when I saw them I knew they would be perfect."

Harlyn grabbed the box and lifted off the lid. She audibly gasped and clutched her hand to her chest. "Oh my god, Meg. They're gorgeous."

"Swarovski blue pear drop earrings. They always say you need something old, something new, and something borrowed on your wedding day. I know you're wearing your mom's necklace and the hair clips in your hair are borrowed from Gwen, so it seemed fitting that I would fill in the blue void." I wanted Harlyn to know I was happy she was marrying Remy. I didn't want to be known as the evil mother-in-law or anything.

"You didn't need to do this, Meg." Harlyn glided her finger over the large blue crystal. "These are way better than the blue underwear I was going to wear."

"Keep those. I'm sure Remy will appreciate them," Marley chuckled.

Fayth high fived Marley. "Amen to that. You know the guys are always more interested in what's beneath the dress, anyway."

Harlyn put the lid back on the box and held the box to her chest. "Thank you, Meg. You didn't need to do that, but you have no idea what it means to me."

I shrugged. "Maybe you can start the tradition of giving them to your first born when they get married or something like that." It sounded lame coming out of my mouth, but I did hope Harlyn would start the tradition.

"I definitely will," she whispered. Harlyn shot up out of the chair and Gwen shouted in protest.

"What the hell, woman? I'm trying to make you pretty."

"Sorry," Harlyn laughed. "It seemed like the right time to hug my future mother-in-law."

Gwen threw her hands up in the air. "Well, get on with it then."

I hugged Harlyn and tried not to cry.

I tried for about five seconds before I was a blubbering idiot rambling on about having a daughter finally.

I was a nut, but I was one happy nut.

*

Chapter Ten

Lo

Meg walked with Remy down the aisle without crying.

She managed to only shed a few tears when he kissed Harlyn.

But when it came time for the mother/son dance, she lost it.

Remy danced slow circles with Meg while she sniffled, babbled, and stroked his cheek from time to time.

And, Remy let her.

"Hey, Lo." Turtle sat down next to me. "You're still okay with watching Jonas for us tonight?"

I nodded my head and smiled. "Sure thing, brother."

Turtle sighed. "Thank god."

I clapped him on the shoulder. "Take a deep breath. You and Mal are perfect for each other."

"I think that and so do you, but does Mal?"

"She would have left you long before now if she didn't."

"Dada!" Jonas ran across the dance floor with Mal chasing behind him. "Can we dance now?"

Jonas shouted it loud enough and just as the music faded out. Everyone laughed and Turtle scooped him up in his arms. "Yeah, twerp," Turtle laughed. "We can dance now."

The DJ announced it was time to party and the floor was swarmed with people ready to dance.

Meg fought her way through the crowd and collapsed into my lap. "I'm dying, handsome."

"No, you're beautiful, babe." I hadn't had much time with Meg alone since I had seen her walk down the aisle with Remy. She may not have been in black, but she looked absolutely stunning in the dark plum dress.

She hiked up her dress and lifted her foot. "These things are what's killing me. I don't know how Gwen manages to wear them for an hour, let alone eight." She toed them off and sighed. "Freedom," she moaned. She dropped the shoes on the floor and wiggled her toes. "Torture devices," she mumbled.

She leaned back in my arms and sighed.

"Uh, I forgot to mention something to you."

"Lay it on me, handsome. I'm about to drink a six pack of wine coolers and dance my ass off. Nothing is going to phase me."

"I promised Turtle we would watch Jonas for him tonight."

Meg dropped her head back on my shoulder. "Lo," she moaned. "How am I supposed to drink a six pack of Jamaican Me Happy when I'm supposed to be an adult?"

I brushed her hair back from her face. "You don't have to worry about watching him. He'll be running around with the rest of the kids all night and crash out before you know it."

Meg rolled her eyes. "You are such a man." She sat up and turned to look down at me. "Why does Turtle need us to watch Jonas for him and Mal?"

I smiled and pointed to the side of the dance floor where Turtle and Mal were dancing with Jonas.

Meg turned and gasped when Turtle got down on one knee. She glanced back at me with tears in her eyes. "You knew this whole time he was going to ask Mal to marry him and you didn't tell me?"

I shrugged. "You had a lot of things going on. Figured you would find out about it when Mal did."

"Liar. You just didn't want me to ruin the surprise."

"That too," I drawled.

Jonas came running over with Mal and Turtle trailing behind.

"Mama Meg!" Jonas yelled. "Dada said I get to stay with you tonight!"

Meg scooped him up in her arms and hugged him close. "You do! We're gonna dance our butts off and then we're going to have a sleepover."

Jonas scrambled out of her lap and back onto the dance floor.

"Are you sure you're okay with Jonas staying with you?" Mal asked.

Meg stood up and shook out her dress. "Girl, I am more than okay with watching him. You and Turtle just got engaged!"

Mal screeched and held out her hand. A large stone gleamed on her finger and Mal's bright smile rivaled the shine of the diamond. "Finally!"

Meg and Mal hugged then gushed over the ring.

Turtle sat down next to me.

"Told you she was going to say yes. You had nothing to worry about."

Turtle nodded his head. "You always do seem to be right, brother. I guess that's why you're the president, right?"

"Been around for a while. I know the love of a good woman and I can see it when someone else has it. You've got it, Turtle. Don't let it go."

Turtle looked at Mal and smiled. "I don't plan on it."

Meg came over to hug Turtle and congratulate him. "It's about damn time," she scolded him. "Who would have thought you were going to be the last one to finally take the plunge."

"I watched all of you guys fall. Was trying to figure out the right way to do it without all the drama you guys had." Turtle reached for Mal and put his arm over her shoulders. "You guys good with us taking off now?"

I nodded my head. "All good. Meg is going to get drunk and I'll keep an eye on the kids."

Meg slapped me. "I am not going to get drunk." She turned to Mal. "Just tipsy."

Mal and Turtle managed to grab Jonas off the dance floor and give him a hug and kiss.

I pulled Meg into my arms and buried my face in her neck. "I think all of the original members of the Devil's Knights finally found their happy endings, babe."

She glanced over her shoulder at me. "You think so?"

I pressed a kiss to her lips. "I fucking hope so."

*

Chapter Eleven

Meg

"All the kids are sleeping."

I lifted my head off the armrest of the couch. "It's about time. I'm way too old for kids under the age of eighteen."

Cyn cackled and patted me on the head. "You're funny. I'm the same age as you and I have a good seven years before eighteen, and I have a feeling the teen years are going to be the hardest with Micha."

"Well, I have a twenty-eight-year-old who just got married. Three is an age I can't quite keep up with anymore." I loved Jonas to death, but I was thankful we were only watching the cutie overnight. I was going to need to take a good ten-hour nap to recover from the wedding and chasing after Jonas for three hours.

"We're heading home."

I peeked my head over the top of the couch and saw Gravel with his arm over Ethel's shoulders. "Did you have a good time?" I asked.

"The best," Ethel smiled. "The cake was amazing and as with any Devil's Knights party, the booze flowed like water."

That was the damn truth. "Drive safe and maybe we can meet for breakfast in the morning. We'll have Jonas with us."

"Let's plan on it." Ethel threaded her fingers through Gravel's and they strolled out the front door.

"I want to be Ethel and Gravel when I grow up," Paige sighed. "They're so sweet together."

Suddenly I remembered what Lo had told me a couple of days ago. I jackknifed up off the couch and gasped. "Oh my god! I forgot to tell you guys. Lo totally walked in on Gravel giving it to Ethel the other day."

"No!" Cyn gasped.

Fayth, Gwen, and Paige giggled while Marley's jaw dropped. "Good god, that is awful!" She shook her head. "I do not need to think of Gravel doing… well.. Anything. As far as my mind goes him and Ethel sit at home watching Jeopardy and drinking tea."

"I'll take delusional for five hundred, Alex," Fayth snickered.

Marley flipped her off. "Monks. Ethel and Gravel are monks in my head."

Cyn stood up and stretched her arms over her head. "We should totally head to bed. The kids are going to be up at the butt crack of dawn even though they went to bed after their bedtime."

I made the familiar walk to Lo's room and found him already lying in bed. "Fancy meeting you here, handsome."

Lo chuckled and rested his arms behind his head. "I was wondering when you were going to come to bed."

"I was waiting to make sure none of the kids woke up." I had actually been too lazy to get my butt off the couch.

"Get ready for bed, babe. It was a long day."

I gave him a thumbs up. "Normally I'd argue with you just because I like to get you riled, but you're so right it's not even funny." I walked to the bed and turned my back to Lo. "Unzip me." My dress loosened as he slowly unzipped the zipper, and it pooled at my feet.

"Babe," he growled. "Did you seriously not have underwear on all day?"

I glanced over my shoulder at him. "Maybe," I whispered coyly.

He slapped my ass. "Get ready for bed. I'm waiting." He laid back and put his hands back behind his head.

"Give me ten minutes and I'm all yours." I was tired, but I was never too tired for Lo.

I was splashing water on my face when Lo's phone rang. I grabbed the towel and patted my face. It wasn't odd for Lo's phone to ring this late, but it also wasn't normal.

"Babe," Lo called.

The tone of his voice made me freeze. Something wasn't right.

Something had happened.

I dropped the towel on the ground and dashed out of the bathroom.

Lo was pulling a shirt over his head and the lights were all on.

"What is it?" I demanded.

Lo's eyes connected with mine and every bad thing that could have happened flashed through my head.

Was it Remy? Did something happen to Ethel and Gravel?

"There was an accident."

My heart plummeted to my feet. "Who?" I whispered.

Lo's eyes dropped to the floor. "Turtle and Mal." He lifted his head. His eyes were glazed over and a lone tear streamed down his cheek. "It's bad."

*

Chapter Twelve

Lo

"This is everything they came in with."

I grabbed the small plastic bag and gripped it in my hand. "That's it?" My voice was weak and I could barely get the words out.

The nurse nodded her head. "Nothing was recovered at the scene and that's all they had on them."

I nodded my head. "Thank you." What else do you say when you're handed a small bag with the last belongings to one of your best friends and his girlfriend?

Fiancée.

Mal had just become his fiancée hours before, and now they were both dead.

A quick glance in the bag showed a diamond ring, wallet, and a rumbled receipt. "Wait, nurse," I called.

She spun around and glanced back at me.

"What about his cut?"

She wrinkled her nose. "Excuse me?"

"His leather vest. Do you know where that is?"

"Oh. I suppose it's in the pile of dirty and torn clothes. I'll see if I can find it. If it was in good shape, they probably would have put it in the bag though." She headed back into the area where Turtle had been.

I leaned against the wall and sunk down till my ass hit the cold, hard floor.

With one phone call, everything had changed.

One of my brothers was gone, and there was nothing I could do to change or fix it.

"King."

Rigid and Demon pushed through the swinging doors into the ER hallway. Rigid had two cups of coffee in his hand and Demon had one.

"Got you a coffee, brother." Rigid handed me the cup.

I took it and set it next to me. "Thanks," I mumbled. Rigid and Demon had made the ride to the hospital with me, while the rest of the guys stayed back with all the women and kids.

"So what now?" Demon asked.

That was a good fucking question. There were so many things that needed to be done that I had no idea where to start first. "Uh, well…" I trailed off.

"Is this it?" The nurse walked toward us with Turtle's cut in her hands. "I wasn't sure if this was it or not, but I didn't know what else it could have been."

I stood up and grabbed the ripped and tattered leather from her. "Yeah, this is it." Half of the patch on the back was caked with dirt and the leather toward the bottom was basically disintegrated.

"Fucking hell," Rigid sighed. "Nothing stands a chance against hard asphalt when you're going sixty miles an hour and get nailed by a deer."

I closed my eyes and tried not to imagine what raced through Turtles mind when that deer jumped out in front of him.

That could have been any of us.

I cleared my throat and squeezed the coat in my hands. "Let's get back to the clubhouse. It's been a long night, and the sun is going to be up before we know it."

We made our way out of the hospital, none of us talking, but the events of the night weighed heavily on each of us.

We had started the day celebrating Remy and Harlyn getting married, then Turtle popping the question to Mal, and it ended with a shock that rocked the clubhouse to the core.

My hands shook as I gripped the handlebars of my motorcycle and I glanced over at Rigid and Demon.

We all felt the void.

Turtle was gone, and he wasn't going to come back.

Life changed as we knew it, but none of us knew just how much it was going to change.

*

Meg

My fingertips brushed Jonas's sandy blonde hair from his forehead and sighed.

I didn't want him to wake up.

Once he woke up, his whole world was going to be crushed.

"Babe."

My eyes snapped to Lo standing in the doorway of the room all the kids were sleeping in. He had left two hours ago, and I have never been more relieved to see his handsome face.

"Lo," I croaked. I had been trying to hold back the flood of tears that had been threatening to flow since Lo got a call from the state trooper.

"Let him sleep, babe. The sun is going to be up soon."

I looked back down at Jonas and stroked my fingers over his forehead. "Sleep well, little man." The morning sunlight was only going to bring heartbreak.

Lo pulled the door shut behind me when I finally tore myself away from Jonas. I launched myself into his arms and wrapped my body around him.

He lifted me into his arms and carried me back to our bedroom. I buried my face in his neck and kept my arms wrapped around him when he tried to lay me down in the bed.

"Babe, you gotta let me go," he whispered in my ear.

I shook my head. "No. I'm not letting you go. At least not right now." The tears I had been trying so hard to hold back were now flowing and soaking Lo's black tee.

"Got my boots on, babe. Let me get them off and then I'll be right back to you."

My arms tightened around him and I hiccupped. "Sleep in them."

Lo chuckled. "Thirty second, babe." He grabbed my arms and pulled them from around his neck and I dropped onto the bed.

I sniffled and wiped my nose with the back of my hand. "Hurry."

Losing someone close to you intensified the feeling to never let go of the people you loved.

Lo toed off his boots, draped his cut over a chair, and turned off the lights. He pulled his shirt over his head as he made his way back to the bed and tossed it on the floor. He popped open the button on his jeans, dropped them to the floor, and climbed back into bed with me.

"Not even thirty seconds," he mumbled. He gathered me into his arms, rolled us under the covers, and I laid my head on his chest.

"Are you okay?" I whispered into the dark.

His voice was low and gruff. "Not even close."

I pressed my body as close to him as I could get. I was a complete mess too, but Lo needed me more right now.

The urge to want to crawl under his skin and take away all of his pain was intense and all consuming. "It's gonna be okay, honey."

"Is it?" he whispered. "There's a three-year-old sleeping just down the hall. He doesn't have a mom or dad anymore, Meg. He's gonna wake up, and somehow you and I are going to have to tell him he's never going to see them again."

My throat tightened, and I fought to pull in a breath. "He… he's gonna…" I choked on my words and clamped my eyes shut. "He's gonna be okay because he has us, Lo. He has you."

Lo buried his head in my hair and a sob racked his body. I scooted up, pulled out of his arms and wrapped my arms around him. Lo was the one who was always there for me when I fell apart, but now it was my turn to be there for him.

The strongest man I had ever known was crumbling in my arms and the only thing I could do was hold on and pray to god that everything was going to be all right.

*

Chapter Thirteen

Lo

"He's three, Lo."

I crossed my arms over my chest and watched Jonas play with his trains. "I know that, Meg. I'm just worried that he doesn't understand what we told him."

"He doesn't Lo."

I glanced over at Meg. "Are you trying to make me feel better about this?"

She nodded her head. "Yes."

"Try harder, babe." Nothing was going to make me feel better about any of this. "Turtle and Mal are dead, Jonas doesn't have parents, and we have no idea what is going to happen with him." Add on top of that we are planning two funerals. All things that none of us knew how to deal with.

"Well, it's barely been forty eight hours since the accident, Lo. You can't expect everything to just figure itself out." She sipped her coffee and kept her eyes on Jonas. "Roxanne, Mal's partner at their law firm, will be here in a little bit."

"And why is she coming here?" I asked.

Meg shrugged. "She said there were some things she needed to go over with us."

"You think we can talk to her about what is going on with Jonas?" Was he going to go into foster care? Did Mal have family that was going to want to raise Jonas?

Meg glanced at me. "I planned on it." She grabbed my hand and threaded her fingers through mine. "We'll get it all figured out, honey."

I squeezed her hand and pulled it to my lips. I pressed a kiss to the back of her hand. "Wouldn't be able to do this without you, babe."

She smiled sadly. "I just wish we didn't have to do any of this. I'd give anything to have Turtle and Mal back."

"You and me both," I whispered.

She sighed and rested her head on my shoulder. "So you got everything squared away with the funeral home?"

I nodded my head. "Yeah. Service will be Thursday. We're doing everything here at the clubhouse. Not sure if Mal would have liked that, but I know it's what Turtle would have wanted."

"He was always here, you know? Even when you and I first got together. He was only a prospect, but you couldn't tell."

"What are you talking about?" I chuckled. "Demon and Gambler had him wash their bikes every day for four months. The only reason they told him to stop was because he was taking off the paint with all of the scrubbing. I can't tell you how many times Rigid had him dye his hair." I shook my head and smiled. "Turtle did it all, too. Never complained. Never said no. He was the epitome of the perfect prospect."

76

"I can't tell you how many times he put up with Cyn and I getting drunk. Remember the time I fell on him behind the bar?" Meg laughed and shook her head.

"I think there was more than one time that you fell on him when you were drunk." Turtle was always there for the girls. He was always there for everyone.

"Mama Meg!" Jonas held up his train. "Wanna play?"

Meg jumped up without a thought and dropped onto the floor with Jonas.

She knew what to do with him. She knew how to make him feel like he wasn't alone. She was what he needed right now.

"King," Gambler called. He was behind the bar and had a row of shot glasses in front of him. "For Turtle."

I ambled over to the bar and grabbed a shot. "Is this that nasty ass shit he liked to drink by the bottle?" I laughed.

Demon nodded his head and lifted the shot to his nose. "Sure the hell is," he grunted. He wrinkled his nose in disgust and held it away from him. "How the hell he drank rum mixed with Worcestershire sauce is fucking beyond me."

Rigid grabbed a shot. "Crazy fucker said it tasted like a fucking steak."

"Such a shame that Gravel is going to miss this," I laughed.

Gambler held up a shot. "Don't worry, I saved him one."

Rigid called for Slider and we all gathered around the bar.

We all raised our glasses, and everyone looked to me.

I cleared my throat. "To Turtle. The best brother we ever had. May we all be half the man he was."

Everyone grunted their agreeance and we all drank the offending shot.

"God damn," Rigid grimaced. "He was one hell of a guy, but he had some weird fucking tastes when it came to what tasted good."

I set my glass on the bar and grabbed a beer from Demon. I sat down on one of the stools and popped open the top. My eyes were on Meg. She was on her hands and knees pushing Jonas's train around while he directed her where it needed to go and when it needed to stop.

Rigid and Slider sat on each side of me. "So how did everything at the funeral home go?" Rigid asked.

I shrugged and took a long pull from my beer. "As good as can be expected when planning to bury your friend." The words were so easy to say, but the feeling they gave me was stronger than a current trying to pull me under.

The door to the clubhouse opened, and who I assumed was Roxanne walked in.

"Who's the suit?" Demon asked.

I drained my beer and set it on the bar. "Chick who worked with Mal. She's here to talk about some stuff." I nodded to Rigid. "Think you could keep an eye on Jonas for me?"

Rigid tipped his head to me. "You got it. The kids are watching a movie with Cyn. I'll wrangle him in there."

Meg playfully chased Jonas over to us. "Time for the grownups to be boring," she sang out.

Rigid grabbed Jonas and swung him up in his arms. "Let's go see what Cyn is up to, little dude."

"I wanna stay with Mama Meg," Jonas insisted.

Rigid screwed up his face and crossed his eyes. "You don't want to hang out with me?" he asked with a fake lisp.

Jonas giggled happily and laid his hands on either side of Rigid's face. "You're silly."

"Henk ew," Rigid replied.

Jonas let off another peel of laughter and Rigid carried him down the hallway before he realized he was leaving Meg.

"You ready?" Meg asked.

"As ready as I can be." At this point I was just rolling with the punches and hoped the next punch didn't completely knock me out.

*

Chapter Fourteen

Meg

"Did I leave you speechless?"

Speechless wasn't the right word.

I was downright dumbfounded. "Us?" I whispered.

Roxanne grabbed the papers in front of her and turned them to Lo and I. "Mal and Turtle both named you as who they want to take care of Jonas if something were to ever happen to them."

Megan Birch (Grain) and Logan Birch.

Right there in writing.

Lo and I were supposed to be the ones to take care of Jonas.

What???

"There isn't any family they wanted to take care of Jonas?" Lo asked.

Roxanne shook her head. "I asked them the same question when they drew up their wills two years ago, and they were both very specific that they wanted you two to take care of Jonas."

I glanced over at Lo, and his face was white as a sheet and he was staring at the paper as if he could change what the papers said.

"So that's it?" I whispered. I glanced up at Roxanne. "Jonas is ours?"

Roxanne shrugged. "Technically all of this will have to go through courts and what not, but yes, Jonas is now in your custody. The only reason a judge would not agree with Mal and Turtle's wishes is if you two were unfit or dead." She grabbed the papers back and tucked them in a manila folder. "Neither of those are true." Her voice had cracked on the word dead and I finally saw Roxanne as a person and not just a lawyer reading off a piece of paper.

"I'm sorry," I blurted out.

Roxanne looked startled. "About?"

"You lost a friend too. You saw Mal almost every day."

She cleared her throat and handed the manila folder to me. "She was my coworker." Her eyes darted down to the table in front of her. "And my friend."

"So what do we do next?" Lo asked. "Can we hire you to take care of everything for us? We really have no idea what we're doing." Lo was clueless to the fact Roxanne was hurting just as much as we were.

Roxanne nodded her head and her lawyer mask slid back into place. "I can represent you with all the filings and hearings. These things tend to move at a snail's pace so if you don't hear from me, just know I'm waiting as well." She gathered up her papers and put them back in her briefcase. "Do you know when the funeral will be?"

"Uh, it'll all be here on Thursday. Five o'clock it all starts." Lo grunted.

"Oh, not at the funeral home?" Roxanne asked.

I shook my head. "With both Mal and Turtle being cremated, it felt right to have it here at the clubhouse since there won't be caskets."

Roxanne smiled sadly. "Mal would like that. Turtle and her were complete opposites, but she loved talking about the club and how you guys had become here family."

"We felt the same way." I choked on my words and fought back tears. "We loved having her around."

Roxanne pressed her lips together and sniffled. "I'll see you guys Thursday. I'll let you know if anything comes up before then."

Lo and I said our goodbyes to Roxanne and watched her walk out the door.

"Did that just happen, babe?" Lo asked softly.

I looked down at the folder in front of me. "For a split second yesterday I hoped Jonas could just stay with us, but now that it's a reality, I'm freaking out at the fact that I'm going to go through the toddler years and everything else again." I glanced at Lo. "I have a twenty-seven-year-old who just got married, and now I have a three-year-old." This was all so crazy that I just wanted to laugh.

Seventy-two hours ago I was a married woman living her best years with a grown son who called three times a week.

Now was I forty-six with a three-year-old.

Holy shit.

"I'm forty-five and have a three-year-old."

A laugh escaped my lips. "When Jonas graduates high school, we'll be in our sixties." I buried my face in my hands and laughed hysterically. "We're gonna pull up to the school with our walkers and oxygen tanks."

Lo barked with laughter. "Speak for yourself, babe. I'm younger than you."

"By a year," I wheezed. "Oh my god, Lo, we're gonna be the old parents on the field trips."

"You are going to be the old parents on the field trip." I folded my arms over my chest. "I'm gonna leave all of that up to you."

I quirked my eyebrow at him. "Oh yeah? What if Jonas says he wants Papa Lo to go with him to the apple farm or the museum?"

"Woman," he growled. "That shit is not going to happen."

I sighed and sat back in my chair. "We'll see about that, handsome." I looked around the clubhouse and smiled. "This has to be the weirdest emotions I have ever felt. I'm sad we lost two of our friends, but I'm happy Jonas won't leave us. He'll have the club as his family."

Lo grabbed my hand. "I'm fucking terrified, babe, but I know I wouldn't want to do this with anyone but you." He pressed a kiss to the back of my hand. "Life has always been crazy since the day I met you, so why wouldn't this be any different."

"I feel like that was kind of a backhanded compliment, but I'm going to accept it and say I love you, too." I scooted closer to him and laid my head on his shoulder. "Tell me this is all a dream, Lo. Mal and Turtle are going to walk through that door and Jonas will have his mom and dad back."

"That is one thing I wish I could do, babe, but I don't think it's going to happen."

I sighed and closed my eyes. "Then I guess it's you, me, and the club raising a three-year-old then."

*

Chapter Fifteen

Lo

"Let's not do this again."

I raised my head and watched Demon walk toward me. He had a bottle in one hand and a lit cigarette in the other.

"What are you doing out here?" I asked.

Demon sat down next to me and tipped the bottle toward me. "Felt like I was fucking suffocating in there. Needed some air."

I grabbed the bottle and took a swig. "Same," I grunted.

The memorial service was over and now everyone was hanging around reminiscing about Turtle and Mal while alcohol flowed freely trying to help numb everyone's pain. Jonas had been glued to Meg's side all day, and it killed me to realize that I think he was finally understanding that his mom and dad weren't coming back.

"So, now what?" Demon asked. He stared into the darkness and took a drag off his cigarette. "We go back to normal but with a huge hole where Mal and Turtle used to be?"

Demon's words stung deep, and I held my breath. Tears had been threatening to fall all day, but I had to be the strong one for the club. I had to be the one who saw the hope we all needed too much.

I had to be strong, but my strength was wavering as the day dragged into night.

"He loved this club with everything he had, King." Demon laughed flatly. "Hell, I think he loved this club more than anyone."

"We were his family," I choked out. "We were there when he didn't have anyone, and in return he was there for us for the rest of his life. I could always rely on Turtle. No matter what, when, or how, I knew he would be there as soon as I called him. I didn't know it then, but now I know he was the best guy I ever knew. He knew what this club stood for, and he protected it fiercely."

Demon clapped me on the shoulder and I couldn't hold it back anymore. I couldn't stop the tears from falling.

Turtle was gone, and nothing was ever going to bring him back.

*

Meg

"Come to bed, Lo."

"I can't." His eyes remained on Jonas as he lay sleeping in his bed.

Remy's old bed that was now his.

"He's not going anywhere, honey. You need to sleep just as much as he does."

It was half past midnight, and Lo had been watching Jonas sleep for over half an hour. The memorial service at the clubhouse had still been going when we left after eleven, and I expected it to go into the morning.

Lo had insisted we leave to get Jonas into bed and not sleeping on the couch in the common room.

"Just a few more minutes," he insisted.

I sighed but knew I wasn't going to get him to move. "I'll be waiting for you."

Fifteen minutes Lo finally came to bed. He left our door wide open and the hallway light on.

"You can turn the hallway light off, honey."

Lo pulled his shirt over his head and tossed it on the floor. "It stays on. If he wakes up in the middle of the night, he won't be scared."

I closed the book I was reading and laid it on the nightstand. "It was a long day. I doubt he's going to wake up much before ten o'clock."

"We should get one of those walkie talkie things." He popped the button on his jeans and pulled them off.

"Uh, for what?" I cocked my head to the side. "Is that some new sex lingo the kids are using?"

Lo scoffed and shook his head. "Not that I know of. I'm talking we should get one for Jonas's room."

"Oh." Now I knew what he was talking about. "A baby monitor?"

Lo flipped our bedroom light off and crawled under the covers next to me. "Yeah. That way if he wakes up, we'll know."

I laughed and scooted closer to him. "You do know we live in a small house where he is literally less than twenty-five feet away from us, right?"

"Walls," he muttered.

I laid my head on his shoulder and tipped it back to look at him. "He'll be fine, Lo. I promise."

"That's a promise you know you can't keep. We all know that after this week."

"Lo," I whispered. I laid my hand on his cheek. "We're all gonna be fine. I know it doesn't seem like it, but we are. We just have to make the most of the time we have together."

"I love you, babe. More than I ever thought I could love someone."

I smiled softly. "You wanna know something?"

"You're not gonna tell me that you love me?"

"That love you feel for me? You're gonna feel that tenfold for that little boy next door."

He pressed a kiss to the palm of my hand. "That doesn't seem possible."

"It is. I feel it for Remy." I winked. "I think you're already starting to feel it for Jonas seeing as you refuse to turn the hallway light off."

"But what if that's not enough, babe? What if that love you're talking about isn't going to be enough to replace Mal and Turtle?"

"Oh, sweet Lo. You just made me fall in love with you all over again." I scooted up and pressed a kiss to his lips. "Just by you worrying about it means that it is going to be enough. Just trust me."

"Guess I can do that." A smile spread across his lips. "Been doing it for ten years, what's another ten years?"

"I only get ten more years?"

He wrapped his arms around me and pulled me close. "I like the ten-year lease option."

"Lease!" I squawked. "You own this ass, just like I own yours."

"Shh," Lo chuckled. "We don't want to wake him up."

I rolled my eyes. "But you have the hallway light on. That makes it all right."

"You really think being sassy is a good idea for you this late at night?"

89

There was my playful Lo. I hadn't seen him the past week. "You like the sass."

"That I do, babe. I can't really deny that at all."

I sighed and laid my head back on his shoulder. "Things go back to an even keel now, right?"

Lo grunted. "I don't know about that. You just became a parent for the second time, and I'm brand new at all of this."

"You're gonna do great," I whispered.

"Just taking my cues from you, babe. You did a damn fine job with Remy."

"I did, didn't I?"

Lo pinched my side and I yelp. "Try to be a little modest," he smirked.

I snuggled back into his side. "You better be thankful that I'm too tired to show you my actual sass."

"Raincheck?"

I closed my eyes and patted him on the chest. "Definite raincheck."

"Sleep tight, babe."

I drifted off to sleep snuggled in with the man of my dreams, dreaming about how much everything was about to change.

*

Chapter Sixteen

Lo

"He's three, Meg. What the hell does he need to go to school for?"

Meg thrust the paper in my face. "He's going to be four in a month, Lo, then two weeks after that, school starts. It's just for half a day. I remember Mal talking about it. She wanted him to go to PreK."

"How is that even a thing?" I grunted. What the hell was he going to do in school? Draw pictures, take a nap, and eat a snack? He could do all of that at home with us.

Meg and I were sitting at the kitchen table finishing our breakfast while Jonas was sprawled out on the couch watching Mickey Mouse.

Meg rolled her eyes and withdrew the paper from my face. "It's a thing because the school says it's a thing." She read over the paper and tossed it on the table. "I'm gonna have to call the school today. Enrollment was last week."

Last week when Jonas's parents died and Meg and I became parents. That last week. It felt like it was ages ago, but the pain from it was still very much there.

"Come on, babe. You really think he needs to go to school? He's super young."

Meg nodded her head. "He is really young, Lo, but it'll be good for him to go to school. Hangout with kids his age and just start learning, well, everything."

"Jonas," I called.

"Yeah, Papa Lo?" he called back.

"You wanna go to school or hangout at the garage with me?"

Jonas's head popped over the half dividing wall of the living room. "Can I do both?"

Meg snickered. "You sure can, because school is only half a day and then you can go to work with Papa Lo the rest of the day."

"You talk to him about this already?" I muttered.

Meg circled her finger above her head. "I would never do something like that, honey, I'm an angel."

"Angel my ass," I growled.

"Papa Lo, you can't say that!"

"Say what?" I grunted.

"I can't say it either," Jonas giggled.

"Ass," Meg pronounced loudly. "Is that the word, Jonas?"

"Yup!" He pointed his finger at me. "Don't say dat."

I poked my finger in my chest. "I can't say it but Mama Meg can say it?"

"Yes." His curled his lip and gave a growl. "Dat's the law." He dropped out of sight in a fit of giggles.

"So how come you get to cuss and I can't?"

Meg shrugged and grabbed her empty plate. "Maybe because I'm Mama Meg?"

"You're something alright, but it ain't got nothing to do with what that little boy calls you."

Meg flipped me off and she flounced over to the sink and dropped her plate in. "You better be careful, or I'll set Jonas on you."

I shook my head and finished my coffee while Meg did the dishes and started a load of laundry.

"You just planning on holding down that chair you're sitting in, or did you actually have something to do today?" Meg set the loaded down basket of laundry on the table and blew a wisp of hair from her face. "With fall coming you could work on the yard."

That sounded like something I did not want to do at all. "Got some things I need to be doing at the shop."

"Right," Meg drawled. "You seem to forget that I know everything going on in the garage seeing as I'm the one answering the phones and writing down all of the work orders."

"Uh, club stuff."

"Logan Birch, you are so full of shit that I'm surprised your eyes aren't brown."

"Jonas," I called. "Meg just said shit."

Jonas popped up again. "I didn't hear her say it, but I heard you say it."

"Not even two weeks and you managed to turn the kid against me," I grumbled under my breath.

Meg shrugged and dried her hands on the dish towel hanging off the stove. "I guess the kid knows who wears the pants in the house."

I moved to the sink and dropped my coffee cup in. "We'll see who has the pants on later tonight." My arms wrapped around her waist and I pulled her close. "Now kiss me so I can get to work."

"You mean hanging out with the club all day," she mumbled. Her arms wrapped around my neck and she leaned up on her tiptoes. "I'm making meatloaf for dinner. Try not to be late."

She pressed a quick kiss to my lips but I pulled her back in before she could pull out of my arms. "You know I'm gonna need more than that, babe."

She huffed but didn't pull out of my arms. Jonas had dropped back down on the couch and all of his attention was on the TV.

"I'm gonna need something to hold me over until tonight."

"What happens tonight?" Meg whispered.

I glanced over to make sure Jonas wasn't watching then delved my fingers into her hair. Her head tipped back and my lips claimed hers.

"Lo," she gasped softly when I finally let her up for air.

"That and a whole lot more is going to happen tonight."

*

Meg

"I want chocolate milk."

I set the white milk in the cart and looked down at Jonas. "We can't get chocolate milk because I have no self-control and it'll be gone before dinner."

"What's self-control?" Jonas asked.

I sighed and glanced at the cooler full of my delicious nemesis. "Self-control is knowing something is bad or wrong, even if it's delicious and not eating or doing it."

"So chocolate milk makes you be naughty."

Chocolate milk contributed to making my butt a few sizes bigger, and I wasn't up to testing the fact if Lo really did love me no matter what. "Yes, that is exactly it. It's so good that I can't say no to it."

Jonas grabbed a bag of potato chips. "What about these?" He smiled widely and shook the bag.

"We can get those because they aren't my favorite. I can say no to those." At least half of the time.

"Can we get a small chocolate milk and I'll hide it from you?"

This is what my life was coming to. Having a three, almost four-year-old, have to hide chocolate milk from me.

I stepped over to the cooler and grabbed a half gallon of chocolate milk. "You know what, we'll get this one and you yell at me if I drink any." I could make Jonas my drill sergeant when it came to eating naughty food. The kid had no filter and blurted anything out that popped into his head. This could totally work.

Jonas grabbed the milk from me and placed it at the bottom of the cart. "Okay. You and Papa Lo can't drink this."

I cringed and tipped my head to the side. Lo didn't really drink milk, but I wasn't sure how that would go over if Jonas told him what he could and couldn't eat. Lo wasn't needing a kid yelling at him to drop the chocolate milk. Even in his forties, the man looked like he was thirty. Half of me loved that about him and the other half wanted to shove a donut in his face and demand he gain a few pounds. "Maybe just me, Jonas. Papa Lo can eat whatever he wants in the fridge."

Jonas grabbed the bag of dinosaur shaped chicken nuggets. "These nuggs are mine."

"Nuggs?" I laughed.

Jonas nodded his head and hugged the chicken nuggets to his chest. "Yes. That's what dad called them."

I ruffled my fingers through his hair. "Well then that is exactly what they are called then." This was the first time Jonas had really mentioned Turtle.

It was so hard for me to figure out what Jonas was thinking or feeling. Three was a tough age to decipher. He could talk and string words into sentences, but putting his thoughts into words was hard. Hell, I was in my forties and still had a hell of a time saying what I was feeling.

On one hand, I wanted him to always think of Turtle and Mal, but then I also didn't want him to always be sad that they weren't here anymore.

The balance between never forgetting about them and moving on with our lives was a tough line to walk.

We weaved our way through the store picking up things that caught our eyes. Jonas helped to unload everything onto the checkout conveyor then crouched in front of the display with tempting last minute items to buy.

These things were another thing that tested my self-control.

"Paper or plastic?" the cashier asked.

"Mama always brought her own bags to the store," Jonas called.

I closed my eyes and tried not to feel like I was about to wreck the environment with my next words. "Plastic, please."

"He's so sweet," the cashier laughed.

I nodded my head and opened my wallet. "He really is, but he also has a knack for making me second guess everything."

The cashier laughed. "My grandson does the same thing. It's nice that you take the time with yours."

I blinked slowly. My hands became clammy and a heat washed over me. "Come again?" I strained.

"It's nice that you get to spend time with your grandson." She smiled at me and continued to scan all of my items.

"Mama Meg," Jonas tugged on my hand. "Can I get this?"

I waved my hand at him without looking. "Whatever you want, baby," I mumbled.

Did I really look old enough to be Jonas's grandma?

I was young.

Well, I at least felt like I was young.

But I had a twenty-seven-year-old.

Jonas was three.

I did the math and cringed. Jonas totally could be my grandson seeing that Remy would have been twenty-three or four if Jonas was his.

I was totally the age to be a grandma.

And now I had a three-year-old that was mine.

This totally called for hitting the gas station on the way home and drinking a six pack of wine coolers once Jonas went to bed.

I was old and didn't realize it.

Facepalm.

*

Chapter Seventeen

Lo

"Pretty sure I was supposed to have my way with you tonight, babe." I scooped Meg up in my arms and carried her to our bed.

"I'm too old for that, Logan."

"Why are you calling me Logan?" I grunted. I laid her on the bed and pulled the covers over her. She was three sheets to the wind and there was no way in hell I was going to have my way with her like that.

"Because we're old, Logan. We need to go by our full names now." She patted her hand to her chest. "I am now Megan Claire Birch." She closed her eyes and tossed her head back on the pillow. "God, I can't handle this."

I pulled my shirt over my head and tossed it in the hamper. "That's not your middle name, and you were fine when I left after dinner to run a couple of errands. I come back to you drunk and babbling about being old. What the hell did I miss?"

She sighed and slapped her hand on the bed. "Claire made me sound older, so I changed my middle name. Keep up, Lo. You missed so freaking much."

I kicked my pants into the hamper and laid down next to her. "Then clue me in, babe."

"I'm. Old. Logan." She enunciated it each word more dramatic than the last and looked to be on the verge of tears.

"Says who?"

"Gloria!"

"Who in the hell is Gloria?" I had been thinking that with Jonas coming to live with us that Meg would cool it on the kooky dramatics, but I was wrong. Once I figured out who the hell Gloria was, I was going to ask her why she thought Meg was old. Maybe Meg might be able to help me figure that out, but from the state she was in right now, I knew all of this was going to be as clear as mud.

"I don't really know if that's her name," Meg sobbed, "but she's got grandkids so I'm sure she has an old name like that. Gloria seems fitting."

"Meg," I muttered. "Try to make a bit of sense here for me, babe." I was trying to follow her rambling, but that was never easy when it came to Meg.

She took a deep breath and draped her arm over her eyes. "I went to the store with Jonas today. Everything was going good. Jonas is going to protect me from the chocolate milk and we now refer to chicken nuggets as nuggs. That is what Turtle calls them."

This is not at all where I thought this story would start. "I have so many questions, but I'm going to wait to ask them until the end." I lifted her arm and looked her in the eyes. "That's not the end, right?"

She scoffed and laid her arm back over her eyes. "Of course not. How crazy do you think I am? It takes more than chocolate milk and nuggs to make me cry."

Some days I think that was debatable, but today was not the day to debate that with her. "Keep going, babe." I still needed to know who in the hell Gloria was.

"So after we got the chocolate milk and nuggs, we made our way to the cashier." She huffed and dropped her arms to her sides. "Gloria."

"Meg." If I didn't keep her focused I knew she was going to go off on another tangent that was just going to leave me with more questions.

"She said it must be so great for me to be able to spend time with my grandson." Her eyes bugged out, and she tossed her hands in the air. "And then I realized that I was old enough to be someone's grandma, and to top it off, I look old enough to be someone's grandma!"

And there it was. Now it all made sense.

I gathered her in my arms and pulled her close.

"Squeezing me is going to give me more wrinkles, Lo!" she squawked.

"Shh, babe. You're gonna wake up Jonas and then I'm not going to be able to show you just how not a grandma that you are."

She huffed and relaxed in my arms. "The only thing that is going to change that is if you can turn back time about twenty years."

"You were married to Hunter and had a seven-year-old twenty years ago."

She smacked me on the chest. "I just mean so I can get my body back that I had then. I'd like to keep you and my life."

"Can't do that, babe. You can't have this life and not have the body to show for it." I ran my fingers up her arm. "Every inch of you is the way that is because of everything you went through to get here."

"I would have liked to have skipped Hunter being an ass to me for like ten years. Pretty sure I'd still be old without that."

"But you never would have left him, figured out who you were as a person, and then met me."

She tipped her head back. "I see the point you are trying to make, and while it is a good point, I would just like to deny the fact that I am old enough to be someone's grandma."

"Any little baby would be damn lucky to have you as their grandma. Just like Jonas is damn lucky to have you, his Mama Meg."

She blew out a raspberry and laid her head back on my shoulder. "I hate when you're all logical and make sense."

"Well, that's better than drinking a six pack of wine coolers and giving yourself a new middle name."

"It made sense at the time," she mumbled.

"So are we over the crisis and I can continue on with the plans I had for you?"

"I suppose," she grumbled.

"Good. Stay here and don't move. I'm gonna shutdown the house and make sure Jonas is asleep."

"I've got six wine coolers in me, Lo. Hurry it up or I'll be out in five minutes."

I rolled into her and pressed a kiss to her lips. "One minute." I rolled back, brought her with me, and slapped her ass. "Now keep that ass awake."

She muttered something about Gloria and ice cream then rolled over onto her belly.

I flipped off all the lights, locked the front and back door, and then pushed open Jonas's door.

He was flat out on his back, arms spread wide, and his mouth hanging open. "Sleeps like his dad," I mumbled out loud.

I pulled his covers over him and tucked his stuffed animal under his arm. He rolled to his side and something fell from his hand and hit my foot.

"What in the world?" I grabbed the object and was surprised as hell to pick up a purple and black lighter. What in the hell was Jonas doing with a lighter?

I searched around him to make sure he didn't have any more lighters or things to destroy the house with and pulled his door halfway shut.

"That was way longer than a minute," Meg complained.

I tossed the lighter at her. "What in the hell is that?"

She grabbed it and turned it over in her hand. "Um, well, this would be a lighter, Lo."

"It is, Meg. You want to take a guess on where I found it?"

She rolled her eyes and tossed it back at me. "Is this the game you wanted to play with me tonight after Jonas went to sleep? My tipsy brain isn't into this, Lo."

"I found it in Jonas's room, Meg. He rolled over, and it dropped out of his hand."

"What?" she squawked. "Where did he get that?"

"Seeing as you were the one who was him all day, I figured you would be the one to better help figure that out." A three-year-old and a lighter didn't mix. Especially since neither Meg nor I smoked.

"There's gotta be a reason why he-." Meg's mouth dropped. "Oh no."

"Oh no, what, babe?"

She scrambled out of the bed and pushed me out of the way. She dropped in front of the sink and pulled open the cabinet doors. "It can't be," she muttered. She pulled out all the plastic bags she squirrelled away down there and looked in each of them.

"Meg, what in the hell are you doing?"

She pulled a crumpled receipt from the bag and read it out loud. "Pasta, chicken, cinnamon rolls, eggs, soda, flour, sugar, baking soda, coffee cake, mini muffins, bell peppers, bacon, cat treats, licorice, seven donuts, ligh-." she crumpled up the receipt and tossed it on the floor. "Son of a bitch, I bought him the damn lighter."

"You bought him this?" I held up the lighter. "Are you freaking kidding me, Meg? I've never done this parenting thing before, but I'm pretty sure buying the kid a lighter is a no."

She hung her head and sighed. "We were at the checkout, and Gloria was talking to me about being a grandma. Jonas asked me if he could get something and I was in the denial zone about being old. I told him yes but didn't look at what he wanted."

"Babe."

She tipped her head back and looked at me. "What? I was in a panic, Lo. What did you want me to do?"

"Pay attention to Jonas and not your midlife crisis." Jesus. Meg was a full blown nutcase.

"Papa Lo?"

I spun around and saw Jonas standing in his doorway. He was rubbing the sleep from his eye and holding his teddy bear under his arm. "You're up." Obviously.

"Why do you have my toy?" He pointed at the lighter in my hand. "Mama Meg bought that for me."

"Jonas," Meg moaned.

"This isn't a toy, little dude." I flicked the lighter and Jonas's eyes bugged out at the flame.

"But Mama Meg said I could have it."

"Ugh," Meg groaned. "I did, Lo. You can't be mad at him for it. This was my stupid mistake."

"I'm not mad at him, Meg, but I do need to let him know that lighters aren't toys." I glanced at Jonas. "Even if Mama Meg buys them for you."

"Why are you on the floor?" Jonas asked Meg.

"Because I'm a fool." Meg stood up and shoved all the bags back in the cabinet. "Remy always had questions for me like that when he was growing up. I'm afraid you are going to have a weirdo raising you, Jonas." She slammed the cupboard shut and propped her hands on her hips. "You and Remy can commiserate together when you're older."

Jonas cocked his head to the side. "What's comomsrate?"

"Commiserate," I chuckled, "and that means you and Remy are going to have an awful lot in common."

Jonas smothered a yawn with the back of his hand. "Do I get my toy back?"

I shook my head. "That's a negative, ghostwriter."

"Huh?"

Meg giggled and scooped Jonas up in her arms. "That's just Papa Lo showing his age."

"Hey," I called. "Mama Meg is waaay older than I am."

She slugged me on the shoulder and turned back to Jonas's room. "Sometimes Papa Lo needs to learn to keep his trap shut, right?" she asked Jonas.

"Woman." Meg was treading a thin line.

"Can I sleep in your big bed?" Jonas asked Meg.

"I, uh, well." She glanced at me. "It's up to Papa Lo."

I glowered at Meg. Of course she would leave it up to me to be the bad guy. The joke was going to be on her. "Sounds good to me, little dude. We can put a movie on and chill out."

Meg's jaw dropped and Jonas clapped his little hands together. "Hooray! I've been wanting to jump on your bed for forever."

I held up my hand. "Whoa there, jumpy pants. We're watching TV and falling asleep. Got it?"

Jonas tried to smother his happiness and nodded his head. "Okay." He failed miserable when he looked at Meg and smiled wide.

Meg took him into the bedroom and for the second time tonight I shutdown the house making sure everything was locked up and the lights were off.

I climbed into bed with Jonas laying in the middle of a pile of pillows like a little king while Meg flipped through the TV channels. "Put something good on, babe."

Meg rolled her eyes. "I'm trying, honey."

"Paw Patrol!" Jonas shouted.

"Not tonight, buddy. Paw Patrol is for the daytime. When it's movie time, we gotta find something that we all like," Meg mumbled while she kept flipping. "What about Transformers?" she asked.

"Fine by me." I settled into the pillows and knew I was going to be sleeping soon. With the TV on and Jonas sleeping in our bed, all the plans I had for the night were out the window.

Meg stopped flipping through the channels and tossed the remote on her nightstand. "This is my favorite one," she whispered to Jonas.

Jonas scooted closer to her and rested his head on her shoulder. "Why?" he whispered back.

"Because it has Mark Wahlberg in it."

I rolled my eyes. "Really, babe?"

"Go to sleep, Lo," Meg giggled.

I tried to fall asleep but after fifteen minutes of trying to ignore the movie, Jonas was the first one to fall asleep.

"He's out," Meg whispered.

I turned my head and watched Jonas snore lightly. "He snores like you, babe."

Meg reached over and pinched my leg. "Keep it up, honey, and I'll make sure Jonas sleeps with us every night."

Now that was not going to happen. "I'm a selfish man, babe. I don't mind sharing you now and then during the night, but you gotta know this is not going to be happening often."

"Lo," she hissed. "He's just a little boy. If he wants to sleep with us now and then that's fine."

"Yeah, now and then is good, babe, but I can tell you right now tomorrow night your ass is mine."

Meg huffed. "You can't talk like that when he's sleeping right next to you."

"Not like I'm trying to get fresh with you while he sleeps between us, babe. Just giving you a warning for tomorrow night."

"You're crazy."

I shook my head. "Nah, babe, that is you all the way. You are the one who bought him a lighter for a toy."

"You're never going to let me live that down, are you?"

I looked back to the TV and put my arm behind my head. "Not a chance in hell I will ever let you forget that."

"It's all Gloria's fault," Meg mumbled.

"Yeah, yeah," I chuckled.

Ten minutes later Meg joined Jonas snoring softly, and I glanced over at them.

This was my life now.

Crazy Meg and adorable Jonas.

I was more than okay with this.

*

Chapter Eighteen

Meg

"And what is your relation to the child?"

"I, uh, well…" My brain froze trying to think of what the right word was. My first instinct was to say I was his Mama Meg, but I'm pretty sure that wasn't an option on the paper in front of the school secretary. "I'm his guardian." There we go. At least I hoped that was an option.

"Okay. Registration isn't for another two weeks, but having all of this info now is good to get the ball rolling. We'll send a packet in the mail with everything we'll be needing when you come in." I listened to papers shuffle over the phone for a second before she continued on. "We will be needing his social security number and vaccination record."

I scribbled that down and felt the panic start to sink in. It had been about twenty-five years since I'd done this. Thank god the lady on the other end of the phone was taking pity on me and not treating me like an idiot.

"Well, Jonas," I called after I ended the call. "Looks like you'll be starting PreK this year." As long as I was able to get his social security card and get him into the doctor.

"You and Papa Lo will come with me, right?" he asked.

I dropped my phone on the kitchen table. "Uh, well. For the start of every day, yes, but then you're going to have to be a big boy."

Jonas popped up and rested her arms on the half wall between the kitchen and living room. "I'm not going if Papa Lo can't come."

"Like I said, honey, he can take you to school every day, but he can't stay."

"Why not?" Jonas asked.

"Because he has a job, and he's already been to school. Now it is your turn."

Jonas shook his head. "We can skip my turn. I'm okay with that."

I walked into the living room and lifted Jonas up in my arms. "Oh my god, did you grow overnight?"

Jonas giggled and shook his head. "No, silly."

He was growing. I swear to god in the past two weeks he had at least grown an inch. Turtle and Mal both had been tall, so I had to assume that Jonas was going to be like them. "I'm just gonna have to squeeze you tight to stop you from growing out of my arms."

Jonas wrapped his arms around my neck and laid his head on my shoulder.

"Tired?" I whispered.

Jonas nodded his head. "Yeah."

"No time to be tired," I laughed while I tickled his sides. "We've got brownies to make, a walk to take, and playground equipment to play on."

"We're going to the park?" Jonas exclaimed.

I nodded my head and set him back on the couch. "Yup. Lo said he'll come pick us up from the park when we're done playing and take us to the clubhouse."

"Woo!" Jonas pumped his fist in the air. "Best day ever."

I had to agree with him, though it seemed like lately every day was the best ever. Jonas living with us was completely different from the normal we were used to, but I had to admit the new normal with Jonas was pretty damn good.

*

Lo

"Again," Jonas screeched.

I pushed him high on the swing and stepped to the side next to Meg.

"He's never going to want you stop pushing him." She bumped into me and I wrapped my arms around her shoulders. "You need to do this half as good as you can so you're not stuck pushing him on a swing for four hours."

"Is that your parenting advice?" I chuckled. "Half-ass it?"

Meg laughed. "Yes, I suppose it is."

I sighed and watched Jonas try to pump his legs, stay high as he swung. "Well, I guess I better listen to you since you've done this before. Remy did turn out pretty well with your half-assed plan."

She laid her head on my shoulder and sighed. "I called the school this morning."

It was crazy to think that Jonas was old enough to start school. "How'd that go?"

"Well, we need to get his social security card and into the doctor."

"Which means we need to go through all of those boxes from Mal and Turtle's place."

Meg nodded her head. "Yup."

We had both put off going through them. It seemed like once we went through all of their stuff that it was done. They really were gone.

"We can do it tomorrow."

Meg sighed. "Okay, honey."

"You're doing good with him, babe." Jonas giggled like a loon and hollered for me to push him again.

"We're doing good with him, honey." Meg laid her hand on my chest and raised up on her tiptoes to press a kiss to my lips. "Now go give him another push because you've created a monster."

Jonas shouted when I pushed him again and I glanced back to see Meg had a huge smile on her face.

116

Two months ago Meg and I didn't have a reason to be at a park in the middle of the day, but now we were here having the time of our lives. Life has a funny way of changing in the strangest ways, but in the end it always worked out.

Meg was happy.

Jonas was happy.

And as long as they were happy, you can bet your ass that I was more than happy.

*

Chapter Nineteen

Meg

"I need absolutely everything you can find that has Paw Patrol plastered all over it. Let's move, ladies."

Cyn and Fayth both grabbed carts and headed in opposite directions. I trailed behind Cyn while Marley and Paige followed Fayth.

"Meg?"

I whirled around wondering who the hell would know my name in the party supply store and was stunned as shit to see Cherry.

Cherry fucking Kratter.

She was wearing dark khaki pants and a bright blue Party Supply polo shirt.

"Uh, hi, Cherry."

"Cher," she corrected. "I go by Cher now."

I nodded my head dumbly not knowing what to say.

"So, uh, are you here by yourself?"

I tipped my head to the side. I had no idea how to take that question. Cherry and I were never on good terms and after the Knights killed her brother, I never expected to be standing in a party supply store talking to her. "I've got some girls with me."

Cherry nodded her head. Or I mean Cher. "Well, if you need anything just holler." She walked back toward the registered and I watched her till she was behind the counter.

"Cyn!" I hissed. Where the hell was she when I needed her. It has been over ten years since I had laid eyes on Cherry, and of course when it happened, Cyn was nowhere to be found.

A bird caw sounded loudly.

"Why you bitch," I mumbled under my breath. I moved down the aisle and listened for the caw again.

After two more caws I found Cyn and the rest of the girls two aisles over.

"You knew, didn't you?" I accused Cyn.

Cyn nodded her head. "Did I know she worked here? No. Did I see her before she saw you? Hell, yes. I haven't run that fast in years." Cyn gripped the handle on the cart. "I had my eyes on you two the whole time though. I was ready to pounce if you needed me."

Ready to pounce my ass. Cyn didn't wanna talk to Cherry any more than I did.

"Maybe we should find another place to buy decorations for the party?" Marley suggested.

I shook my head. "They have the best decorations here, and from the brief conversation Cherry and I just had, I don't think she is going to be a problem." I glanced down the aisle toward the cash register. "Though I still don't trust Cher any further than I can throw her."

"Cher?" Cyn snickered.

I couldn't help but smile. "Yeah. She made sure to correct me right away that she goes by Cher now instead of Cherry."

Fayth wrinkled her nose. "Is that supposed to be an improvement?"

Marley snickered. "There is only one Cher in this world as far as I'm concerned." She brushed her hair to the side and licked her lips. "Do you believe in-."

Paige held up her hand. "No, please. Not another horrible Cher impersonation."

Marley flipped her off. "Screw you, I'm great at Cher."

I waved my hands in the air. "Focus, ladies. Now that Cher is at the counter I just want to get the hell out of here. Anything with those adorable puppies on them, grab it and meet at the register. Cyn and I will take this half of the store, you three take that half."

We once again separated with our goal in sight.

Cyn and I grabbed plates, napkins, cups, tablecloths, and a shit on of confetti. "You think this is enough?"

I looked down at the half full cart. "I'm gonna say yes, but I hope Fayth and them were able to find some more decorations."

"Done!" Paige shouted from the other end of the store.

"Welp, let's find out," Cyn laughed.

We met at the register where Cherry was waiting for us.

"Don't leave me," Cyn whispered.

I glared over my shoulder at her. "Oh, you mean kind of like how you left me earlier?"

"My fight-or-flight instinct kicked in. Flight won," she mumbled.

I rolled my eyes. "It's a good thing you're my best friend."

Fayth had her car loaded down with balloons, candy, little toy party favors, and stuffed animals of all the characters.

"They had t-shirts, but I didn't know if you really meant grab everything that had Paw Patrol on it.

I shook my head and grabbed the white stuffed dog. "This is perfect. Jonas is going to freak when he sees the clubhouse next weekend."

"I think Lo and the rest of the guys are going to freak out too," Cyn laughed. "First, we take over the clubhouse with weddings and now we're going to have a four-year-old's birthday party there."

"It works out perfectly for the guys because once the cake is eaten they can go hangout in the garage or something while the kids run around hopped up on cake and soda." Marley grabbed a pack of balloons. "We're gonna need a helium tank for these."

"I can get you one."

We all spun around. I had forgotten that Cherry was literally a few feet away from us.

"Uh, well, thanks," I stuttered.

"We need to get out of here before Cherry realizes that she hates us," Cyn whispered.

I nodded my head. "Totally."

We unloaded both carts onto the counter while Cherry ran to get a helium tank.

"You suppose she went to the back to get her machete?" Fayth asked.

"Machete?" Marley laughed. "Is she from the jungle or something?"

Fayth waved her hand. "Marco was over last night and we watched Jumanji. I have visions of The Rock in my head. Sorry."

Cyn waved her hand. "Girl, you never have to apologize for having The Rock on your mind."

"Amen to that," I mumbled.

"Here we go." Cherry came back with a box in her arms. "I figured one tank would be enough. Am I right?"

I glanced at Cyn. "Uh, sure? We just have a couple packs of balloons to blow up."

Cherry made small talk about her son loving Paw Patrol too while she rang up everything.

All I could do was mumbled my agreement because I was still shocked as shit that Cherry Kratter was talking to us like we were her friends.

She handed me back my change with a huge smile on her face. "Have a great day."

"Was that the twilight zone?" Cyn asked once we were to the car. "That had to have been the twilight zone." She glanced back at the store. "I'm kind of waiting for her to come tearing out of the store yelling at us."

"Definitely seems more fitting than what just happened." I grabbed two bags from the cart and popped the trunk. "Maybe she found god or something."

"Troy just messaged me wondering when we're going to be back to the clubhouse," Marley laughed.

"Are the kids too much for them?" Paige asked.

"I think seven kids it too much for anyone." Fayth helped me load the rest of the bags while Cyn returned both carts to the store.

She came running out of the store with a huge smile on her face. "Get in the car!" she shouted. "We were totally right about Cherry!"

We all got into the car and Fayth started the engine.

"What in the hell are you going on about?" Marley asked.

Cyn was winded from her sprint across the parking lot and held her hand up. "Give me a minute," she panted. She twirled her finger in the air. "Drive," she ordered Fayth.

Paige and I glanced at each other as Fayth pulled out of the parking lot.

"You got about ten more seconds to catch your breath and then you better start talking, woman."

Cyn took two deep breaths. "She hates you." She smiled widely. "She absolutely loathes me."

"What?" Fayth asked. "How in the hell do you know that?"

"Because when I took the carts back in she was at the front register on the phone just going off about us." Cyn cackled. "I don't know who she was talking to, but it was funny as hell. The only reason she was nice to us was because she needs her job."

I shook my head. "I thought she was pretty sincere when she was talking to us." That's what I got for thinking the evil witch could change her ways.

Cyn held up her hand to quiet us. "She said she had all of our men and settled with her sloppy seconds."

"Well, that is some bullshit," Marley laughed. She wrinkled her nose and shook her head. "If Troy or any of the guys were into her before they met us then I have to say that each one of the guys did one hell of an upgrade."

"Amen to that," Paige called.

"Only we could go shopping for decorations for a four-year-old's birthday party and run into a chick who slept with our husbands," I laughed.

"Never a dull moment, right?" Cyn elbowed me in the side.

Now that was the damn truth.

*

Lo

"That thing… with your… tongue," Meg panted. "Please tell me you never did that with Cherry."

I rolled over on my back and tried to catch my breath. "Just had my dick buried deep inside you and the first thing you ask is about Cherry. Thought I was done with that bitch over ten years ago."

"Me too, until she checked me out at the party store today."

"Well, get that dumb chick out of your head."

Meg rolled over onto her side and rested her hand on my chest. "Maybe you need to try one more time to help me forget about her?" she wiggled her eyebrows and her hand slid down my chest.

"The last two times didn't do the trick?"

She shook her head. "One more time and I'm pretty sure I'll never speak her name again."

"Then hold on, babe. It's time to go for another ride."

Meg hummed and wrapped her fingers around my dick. "I like the sound of that."

*

Chapter Twenty

Meg

"We should have gotten another pack of balloons."

Cyn grabbed the last balloon and hooked it to the helium tank. "You gonna run back to Party Supply and get them? I'm sure Cherry would be more than happy to help you."

"Uh, you know what? I think we have just enough." Cyn tied the balloon and handed it to me.

"Thought you might see it that way." Cyn fell back into the couch and kicked her feet up on the coffee table. "Have any of the guys seen this yet?" she asked.

I shook my head and tied the last piece of ribbon to the end of the balloon. "Nope. Lo and the guys took the kids to the park as soon as we got here, and they have strict orders to not come back until four."

Gwen plopped down on the couch next to Cyn. "Are you sure you're not the president of the Devil's Knights?"

"I guess sharing a bed with him has its perks." I winked at Gwen and grabbed a bunch of balloons Cyn and I blew up. "Help me spread these around and then I think we are good to go."

"You think King will let us have the twins birthday party here too? I'd much rather mess up the clubhouse than our house." Paige carried two bowls of chips out of the kitchen and set them on the bar. "Plus, there is an abundance of booze here."

"The bar is closed until seven. I don't need everyone stumbling around at a four-year-old's birthday party. I don't need CPS on my butt before it's official official that Jonas is ours." I set a bunch of balloons on the end table by the couch and looked around the clubhouse. Paw Patrol had thrown up all over and I knew Jonas was going to freak out when he saw it.

"Aw, it's like she's a new parent trying to be perfect," Cyn laughed. "I remember when I was like that with Micha. It lasted for about two years and then I said fuck it."

"Here, here," Fayth laughed. "With Marco I don't even think I lasted a year trying to be the perfect mom." Fayth plopped down on the couch. "It didn't help that I had zero mom friends because you know, the whole my brother being a Banachi."

"How is Leo doing?" Paige asked.

Fayth shrugged. "As good as can be expected. I wish he would settle down, but he's too focused on building his empire. Thankfully he has Apollo and Greer to be his little family since I'm not there."

"You want me to start bringing the food out?" Ethel called.

I dropped the last bunch of balloons on the bar. "Yes, but don't even think about picking up that roaster, Ethel. I'll be there to get it."

Ten seconds later Ethel walked out of the kitchen carrying the exact roaster I had just told her not to touch. "Nonsense. This isn't that heavy."

128

I met her halfway and followed her carefully to make sure she could handle carrying it. "For goodness' sake, Ethel. If Lo would have seen you carry that he would have had my butt in a sling."

Ethel set the roaster full of hot ham and turkey slices on the bar. "I'm old, not dead," she tsked. "Sixty-eight and I still feel like a twenty-year-old."

Thank god for that. With the health scares Ethel had, it was a miracle she still felt young. Hell, the two cancer scares had aged Lo and I.

I plugged in the roaster and chased Ethel over to the couch. "Well, sit down and let us get the rest of the food. You were nice enough to cook everything so the least we can do is set everything out."

Ethel flopped down on the couch. "I was surprised as hell that you let me cook everything." She laughed and shook her head. "Although you did sent me a pretty detailed list of food and recipes, you wanted me to use."

I grabbed the platter of buns and set them next to the roaster. "Most of those specifics were from Jonas. He was dead set on mac and cheese and cheese puffs."

"I figured those were from him, but I kind of figured the rest was you."

I shrugged and headed back into the kitchen. "Hey, as delicious as mac and cheese and cheese puffs are, I figured we needed more than that to eat."

Fayth and Paige helped me grab the rest of the food and by the time it was all out, the bar was covered and I still had to bring the cake out.

That was the one thing I kept to myself. Though I did have Ethel make a cherry and apple pie for dessert backup if anyone wasn't feeling cake.

"Holy hell, Meg. How long did it take you to make that?" Cyn whistled low. "I always forget how amazing you are when it comes to cake."

"I'm only amazing with cake?" I laughed.

Cyn rolled her eyes and helped me lay the cake down on the card table at the end of the bar. "You know what I meant, woman."

I stepped back and looked at the cake. "I really did kick ass with this, didn't I?"

Three tiers that were Jonas's three favorite characters.

Chase. Rubble. Everest.

Who would have ever thought that I would once again know character names for kids shows? I figured those days were long behind me.

"You do know Greta is going to want you to make this cake for her for her birthday but with her favorite characters, right?" Gwen laughed. "Marshall, Skye, and Everest."

I nodded my head. "Her birthday isn't for another four months. That'll give me plenty of time to recoup from this one."

"Troy just called. He said they are on the way home from the park," Marley called.

"Woo," Cyn yelled. "It's almost party time!"

We all ran around making sure everything was ready from the cake, to the food, to making sure there was toilet paper in each bathroom. Never mind me rearranging the balloons ten times until the front door open and Jonas came barreling in.

He skidded to a stop in the middle of the clubhouse and beamed brightly. "Holy cow," he gasped.

"God damn," Lo said under his breath. He was two steps behind Jonas and his jaw dropped to the floor too.

"So, what do you think?" I asked with my arms stretched wide as I turned a slow circle.

"This is amazing," Jonas gasped. His feet came unstuck from the floor, and he ran around stopping to look at something new every five seconds. The rest of the kids piled into the clubhouse and the guys followed behind.

"Sweet Jesus." Demon shook his head. "You guys can't do shit like this because then the rest of the kids start getting ideas that all the parties are going to be like this."

Even Demon knew this was freaking amazing.

Balloons, streamers, and banners were all over while confetti littered the tables and in the corner was a game where you had to put Chase's fire hat on him.

The kids ran around like crazy, grabbing stuffed animals and collapsed on the floor to play. The older kids even seemed to take it all in and think it was pretty cool.

Lo put his arm over my shoulders and pulled me close. "You did good, babe."

I tipped my head back and smiled up at him. "You think?"

He nodded his head. "I know so."

"Then I guess it was worth it to have to deal with Cherry if it meant Jonas was going to have the best birthday party."

Lo chuckled and nodded to the table by the cake. "What the hell are those?" he asked.

I grabbed his hand and pulled him across the room. I grabbed a red hat and plopped it on his head. "That is Chase's fire hat. Everyone gets one."

Lo took it off and looked it over. "This shit is crazy, babe." He put the hat back on his head and looked around. "He's absolutely going to love it."

I crossed my fingers and held them up. "Fingers crossed that he does, because if he doesn't, I've got a couple of costumes you and the guys can put on to spice things up."

Lo shook his head. "There will be no spicing things up for this guy."

I bumped him with my shoulder. "That's what you like to think. If Jonas wants you to play with him, you know damn well that you aren't going to say no."

She was right, but I wasn't about to tell her that. I leaned close and pressed a kiss to her neck. "I get to be Rubble."

She tossed her head back and laughed hysterically. She put her arms around my neck and pressed a kiss to my lips. "You got it, honey."

*

Chapter Twenty-One

Lo

"We gotta go, babe."

"Uh, I'm coming. Just give me one minute." Meg sniffled through the door.

"Pull it together, mama."

"Are we gonna be late, Papa Lo?" Jonas stood behind me with his backpack on and his snack bag in his hand.

I crouched down in front of him and smiled. "We'll be right on time, little dude. I know Mama Meg well, and knew I was going to have to give her a little more time than normal on your first day."

"She doesn't want me to go?"

I shook my head. "She wants you to go, but she's just a little sad that she doesn't get to spend the whole day with you."

"Then I'll stay home."

"No," Meg called from the bathroom. "I'm fine Jonas. I'm just... I'm just a blubbering mess."

That was the damn truth. Meg had warned me last week that when Remy had started school she cried for two weeks. I was hoping she would be able to pull it together better with Jonas.

The first day was proving she was fully going to be a hot mess.

The door swung open and Meg stood there with a cheesy smile plastered on her face. "Let's go to PreK." she sang.

Yup, this was definitely going to be interesting.

*

Meg

I should have shoved more tissues in my bra.

Jonas was sitting in his chair, everything looking huge around him while he looked tiny.

"I'm gonna go grab a drink from the bubbler, babe. You okay?"

I looked up at Lo and nodded my head. "Yup. I'm great."

He eyed me carefully. I was lying right through my teeth. I was a hot mess express right now.

"You look like you're two seconds away from grabbing Jonas and running out the door."

I held up my hand. "Scout's honor that I will not do that today."

He squinted at me. "I would believe that if you were actually a scout."

I nudged him with my shoulder. "Go. I promise I'll be fine." He was only going to be gone for like two minutes. I could totally hold it together for that long.

Lo went in search of the bubbler and I looked around the room at all the parents.

Lo and I were definitely the oldest in the room, including the teacher. She barely looked like she was a year out of school.

This was a complete opposite experience from when Remy went to school. Back then I was one of the youngest in the room and snickered at the parents who were much older.

Oh, karma, you were a slick one.

The guy standing a couple of feet from me scooted closer. "Which one is yours?"

"Uh, Jonas. The one in the red Paw Patrol shirt." Of course Jonas wanted to wear one of the new shirts he had gotten for his birthday. I had been shocked at how many clothing options there were when it came to kids TV shows these days. Again, a complete one eighty from when Remy had been in school.

"Nice. Mine is the one three chairs over. Olivia." She was a pretty little girl with blond hair and glasses.

"She's adorable." I racked my brain for something else to say, but as usual, I had nothing.

"Is he your only child?"

I cleared my throat. I knew I was going to get questions like this. I had just hoped that Lo was going to be around when I got them. "Uh, no. I actually have an older son."

"Third or fourth grade?"

Oh, boy. "At one point he was, but he's actually twenty-seven."

I had never seen someone more shocked before. "Oh, wow. I, uh, wow."

I couldn't help but laugh. "It's a bit of an age gap." I held my hand out to him. "I'm Meg by the way."

He shook my hand and still had no words.

"And your name is?"

"Oh, sorry. Marcus." He dropped his hand and stepped back. "Don't mean to be such a tool. I was trying to imagine what it would be like to raise one child and then basically start over again."

I shrugged. "It's pretty damn fun. I wouldn't trade Jonas for anything in the world."

Marcus sheepishly ducked his head. "I again sounded like a tool. I'm just going to head to the other side of the room and hope I don't say anything else stupid to you." He slunk off to the other side of the room and didn't make eye contact with me.

Lo walked back into the room and stood next to me. "Why are you looking so smug?"

"I just scared one of the parents. Or at least made him feel embarrassed." I looked up at Lo. "And why do you look slightly terrified?"

He shuddered and shook his head. "Pretty sure I just got hit on.."

"You think you did? Are you losing your touch that you don't know when you're getting hit on?" Lo was damn fine. I couldn't blame anyone for hitting on him. Once. If they tried a second time that was when bitchy Meg came out.

Lo ran his fingers through his hair. "Nah, I'm sure I was hit on, but the person who hit on me was a little surprising."

"Who?" I hissed. If it was that young teacher I was not going to be happy.

Lo looked around and lowered his voice. "The principal."

I reared back and tried to hold back my laughter. "Mr. Seth?"

Lo nodded his head. "Yeah."

"But… but he's…" I leaned in super close. "He's married with five kids."

"Guess that doesn't mean much to him."

I stepped back and turned back to watch Jonas. "Is this your way to distract me from being a blubbering mess?" I glanced back at Lo. "If it is, it worked."

Lo shook his head. "I wish it was a fucking joke, babe."

I tried to stay focused on Lo, but I couldn't get my mind off the fact that not only had Lo been hit on, but it was Jonas's principal.

Once the kids got settled, Jonas's teacher gently hinted at the fact that it was time for the parents to hit the road.

Lo and I walked over to Jonas and I knelt down in front of him. "We're gonna take off, buddy. You only have three hours left of school and then Papa Lo and I will be here to pick up. Okay?"

"How will I know how to find you?" Jonas's voice was quiet and I could tell he was a little unsure about Lo and I leaving.

"We asked your teacher earlier where we get you. You'll be right in the front. We'll be there before you even get out of school." Remy also had the same fear of not being able to find me when school let out. Thankfully Jonas only went to school for half a day and there wouldn't be a mad rush to the door.

Lo ruffled Jonas's hair. "Once we pick you up, we'll go grab burgers and ice cream for dinner."

"Really?"

Lo nodded his head. "Yup. All you gotta do is be a good boy for your teacher."

Jonas nodded his head. "I can totally do that, Papa Lo."

"How come you call him Papa Lo?" the little boy next to Jonas asked.

Before Lo or I could open our mouths, Jonas spoke.

"Because he's always been my Papa Lo. My daddy isn't here no more, but I have Papa Lo and Mama Meg to take care of me."

Tears threatened to fall and Lo squeezed my hand.

"That's pretty cool." The boy looked at Lo. "Can you be my Papa Lo if something happens to my mom and dad?"

"Uh, well, I don't think it works that way where you'll get me, but I know your mom and dad have someone who could be like me."

The little boy looked confused and sad.

I elbowed Lo in the side. "Just say yes."

"But yes, I could do that for you. Totally," he added quickly.

The little boys face lit up. "Cool!"

I managed to hug Jonas goodbye with only a few sniffles and a tear or two.

"I'm surprised you didn't break down in there," Lo laughed. He beeped open the locks on the truck and opened my door for me.

"The fact the seemingly straight principal hit on you threw me for a loop." I hopped into the truck and Lo slammed my door.

"Maybe they're in an open relationship and she's okay with him hitting on bikers?"

I scoffed and buckled my seatbelt. "Who knows if that is true, but you would think the guy would at least not hit on the parents of his students."

Lo shrugged and cranked up the truck. "You would think so, babe, but some people just don't care."

"Well," I drawled. "He can keep his uncaring ass to himself."

"I let him know that in so many words, babe."

"What exactly did he say to you?" Lo had only been gone for a couple of minutes.

Lo shifted into reverse and headed out of the parking lot. "Well, I was bent over getting a drink from the bubbler when he grabbed my ass."

"Shut up!" I gasped.

Lo nodded his head. "For a second I thought it was you, but he opened his mouth before I turned around. About shit myself when he asked if I was tardy and wanted to come to the principal's office with him."

"Hell no. You're making this up." There was no way in hell Mr. Seth would be that bold in school."

"Babe, I swear on your and Jonas's life, that man grabbed my ass and wanted me to come to his office for a mid-morning romp."

"So what did you tell him?"

"To fuck off and keep his hands to himself. If he didn't, and I heard about it, I would break both of his hands so he couldn't touch anyone anymore."

I cringed. "Ouch. I bet he didn't like that very much."

"Dirty prick shouldn't be grabbing people, Meg. Don't give a shit if he is the principal of the school. That should be the one person who shouldn't be doing that."

"He say anything back?"

Lo nodded. "He was real quick to offer up an apology and give me some bullshit excuse that he thought I was someone else."

"That was supposed to make it better?" I laughed. "God, Lo. This was not how I wanted Jonas to start his school year. Now we're going to have to report the asshole."

Lo shook his head. "Nah, I think I have another way to teach this asshole a lesson without getting the school board involved."

"Lo, let's not break the law. Just report him to the school board and let them do what they want with him."

Lo pulled into the driveway and shifted the truck into park. "Nope. Doing this my way, babe. I could tell this wasn't this guy's first time being a grabby asshole. He new to the school?"

I bite my lip and nodded my head. "Uh, yeah. This is his first year."

"So I bet that asshole has gotten in trouble before, but it just got brushed under the rug. He's gonna keep doing this bullshit until he gets taught a lesson, babe."

I pushed open my door and jumped down from the truck. "You figured all of that out about him from one hand grab and a couple of words?" I rounded the truck and climbed the porch steps.

"Know his type, babe. I'm gonna take care of it before he fucks with someone who won't tell him no."

"Meg!"

Oh hell. It was Larry.

"Hey, Larry," Lo called.

"Logan," Larry replied. "I was just going to talk to your wife about the poop in my yard."

Lo looked at me. "Something you need to tell me about pooping in Larry's yard?"

I rolled my eyes and shook my head. "Not sure what poop in your yard has to do with me, Larry."

"Because it has to be your dog."

I frowned and shook my head. "Blue died last spring, Larry. If there is poop in your yard from him, then it must be petrified." Old Blue had been seventeen when he died and there was no way in hell he would have been able to make it over to Larry's yard to poop. He barely was able to make it out of the house the last couple of months. I missed that dog something fierce.

"Are you sure?"

Lo chuckled and shook his head. "Yeah, we're positive, Larry. He's buried in the backyard."

Larry propped his hands on his hips and sighed. "Well, then who is pooping my yard, Meg?"

Oh, Larry. He was getting up there in age, and he was getting crankier by the day.

"Well, it wasn't Lo or I so you can cross us off the list of suspects." I pointed toward the blue house on the other side of the street. "Maybe it's the Mitchell's?"

Larry glared at the blue house. "You may be right."

"Welp, have a good day, Larry. Meg and I have some work to do." Lo grabbed my hand and pulled me into the house.

"What work do we have to do?" I laughed. I pulled the door shut behind me and Lo wrapped me up in his arms.

"We don't. I was just trying to get you away from Larry before you set him onto all the neighbors about the poop." Lo tipped his head to the side. "Do the Mitchell's even have a dog?"

I shook my head and laughed. "Nope. Never have. I just felt like messing with Larry. He didn't realize Blue died, so there is no way he is going to remember that the Mitchell's don't have a dog."

"Well, I guess that'll keep him off our backs for a little."

I sighed and rested my head on Lo's shoulder. "How did Larry not remember that Blue died? Didn't he help you dig the hole?"

"Yeah, but I think Larry is getting up there in his age. It's a good thing his daughter moved in with him."

"Yeah," I agreed. "Otherwise I'm sure he would be giving us a lot more hell about everything."

144

"So," Lo drawled. "We have three hours before Jonas is done with school?"

I bite my bottom lip and nodded my head. "Yup."

"I think there might be some things you need to help me take care of in the bedroom." Lo wiggled his eyebrows and brushed his lips against mine. "Quite a few things, actually." Lo dropped the keys on the end table and pulled me into the bedroom.

"Why, Mr. Birch, are propositioning me? I do believe you just had a run in with a principal trying to do the same thing to you." Lo grabbed me around the waist and tossed me on the bed.

"The difference is I know you want me, babe. Principal Grabby-pants is a lawsuit waiting to happen. Or an asskicking that is going to happen." Lo pulled his shirt over his head and tossed it at my face. "Now get your clothes off and stop talking."

I shimmied my leggings off and kicked them to the end of the bed. "Yes sir, Principal Birch."

Lo smirked and dropped his pants to the floor. "You're gonna pay for that one, babe."

A tremor rolled through my body in anticipation. "Promise?"

"Have I ever broken a promise to you yet, babe?"

I shook my head and pulled my shirt over my head. "Nope, so let's not start today."

He grabbed my foot, pulled me to the edge of the bed and in between his legs. I plastered my hands on his bare chest and smiled up at him.

"I'll never get tired of that wonky smile, babe."

I ran my hands up his chest and looped them around his neck. I pulled him down until his lips were a breath away from mine. "I know I should be offended by that, but all those words did was make my loopy heart beat faster and my loopy smile wider."

Lo's lips pressed against mine, a low grumble rumbled from his throat, and his hands skimmed over my back and grabbed my ass. "You're mine, babe."

"Was there ever a thought that I wasn't?"

"Not on my end. I think you might have fought it for a second."

I held up my pointer finger and thumb a centimeter apart in between us. "Maybe for like a nanosecond."

"Worst nanosecond of your life, right?"

I nodded my head and pressed my lips to his. "But we've been making up for it ever since. Lo Daze, baby."

Lo pushed me back onto the bed and covered my body with his. "You're fucking crazy, babe." He brushed kisses across my jaw and up to my ear. "But I wouldn't want you any other way. All. Mine."

Yes indeed, I certainly was.

Stuck in the Lo Daze for ten years and counting.

*

Chapter Twenty-Two

Lo

"His name is George Seth."

Rigid raised his hand and pointed to the picture I handed out. "Uh, pretty sure this is my kid's principal."

I nodded my head. "He is your kid's principal and everyone else's kids at this table."

"Probably something I should have known, right?" Demon asked. "Having twins has fucked with my mind. Can't remember shit besides dumb songs about baby sharks and how much Tylenol I can give the kids."

Rigid chuckled and shook his head. "If it makes you feel better, this is his first year being the principal."

Demon pointed his finger at Rigid. "That actually does make me feel a little better about being a shitty parent."

"If you were a shitty parent, I'm pretty sure Paige would have left your ass a long time ago." Gravel nodded to me. "You wanna clue us in as to why we're looking at a picture of this guy?"

No, I really didn't want to because I knew they were just going to give me shit about it, but they needed to know why we were going to scare the shit out of this guy.

"Anyone of you assholes laughs in the next ten minutes, I'll kick your ass. Got it?" I looked around the table and glared at each of them.

"This is going to be good." Rigid rubbed his hands together and leaned forward in his chair.

I sat back in my chair and tried to figure out where to start. I wish I didn't have to tell these assholes, but I knew they weren't going to let it go until they knew what happened. "Meg and I took Jonas to his first day of school on Tuesday."

"As did we all, although you were the only one who left wanting to kick the new principal's ass," Demon chuckled.

"Everyone but me," Slider clarified. "Marco is past having to take to his first day of school."

"Lucky bastard," Gambler grumbled.

Slider splayed his hands out in front of him. "I was the only one smart enough to find a good chick with an almost full grown kid."

Gravel slapped Gambler upside the head. "Shut up you, assholes. I wanna know what the hell is going on with the principal."

I sighed and continued on. "We took Jonas to his class, did the typical shit with him, and then I went to get a drink from the bubbler."

"Holy shit," Rigid whispered.

"Holy shit what?" Demon looked around the table confused. "What the hell did I miss?"

"Nothing," Rigid laughed, "but I know exactly where this story is going."

"Oh yeah?" I asked Rigid. "Why don't you tell me what happens next?"

Rigid shook his head. "Hell no. I want to hear those words come out of your mouth."

Might as well just get straight to the fucking point. "I leaned over to get a drink from the bubbler, he grabbed my ass, and invited me back to his office."

Everyone froze, speechless.

A low inaudible sound came from Rigid.

Gravel held my gaze and shook his head.

"I knew it," Rigid whispered. "I knew you were going to fucking say that."

"Well, I can tell you right the fuck now that I didn't expect you to say that. I figured you were going to say you caught him beating a kid or coping a feel on a teacher, not fucking you." Gravel shook his head. "Fucking world is going to hell in a handbasket."

"Handbasket, Grandpa?" Demon laughed.

Now it was Demon's turn to get slapped upside the head by Gravel. "You're all a bunch of fucking halfwits, you know that?"

"So why didn't you just haul back and punch the fucker's lights out?" Gambler asked.

"Because that wouldn't have taught him anything. The asshole probably would have denied any shit I had to say to him and would have been able to keep grabbing whoever the hell he wants to."

Rigid raised his hand. "So the new principal is obviously bi who has a wife and five kids who cheats on his wife with any random person who suits his fancy when he walks by?"

"In a nutshell." I laid my palm on the table.

"So we give him a little Devil's Knights justice so he starts acting right?" Gambler suggested.

I nodded my head. "I figured out where he lives. I want Demon and Gambler taking turns watching him for a couple of nights. Figure out his patterns. What time he leaves in the morning, when he gets home, anywhere he goes, I want to know."

"What happens after we figure out all of that?" Gravel asked.

"Then we give principal Seth a house call and show him some Devil's Knights justice."

*

Chapter Twenty-Three

Meg

"I can't believe you bought ass flavored air freshener."

"What?" Lo paused the TV. "I'm pretty sure the bottle said lilac, not ass."

"Lilac is ass." I held up the offending bottle of assy scent. "This is ass scented." I squirted it into the air and fell into a fit of coughing and gagging.

"Well, it's meant for the air, not to be a body spray for you."

I waved my hand in the air and dropped the can into the bathroom garbage. "You're not allowed to buy anything that has a scent to it. You've failed me. It was a good marriage while it lasted."

Lo turned to Jonas who was sitting next to him on the couch. "She's leaving me over a lilac air freshener."

"I know," Jonas mumbled. "She was yelling about it before you got home." His eyes were glued to the TV, and he shoveled a handful of cheese popcorn into his mouth.

"Why didn't you throw it away earlier?" I asked.

"Because I had to keep it as evidence until you got home. You're home, so now it goes in the garbage where it belonged all along." I slammed the bathroom door shut. "It's like you don't know me at all, Lo."

"It's just an air freshener," I heard Lo mumble through the door.

I pulled open the door and pointed a finger at Lo. "An air freshener you know I hate."

Lo scooted to the edge of the couch. "Babe."

"Don't you babe me, Logan."

He stood up stood in the doorway to the bathroom. "You know what this is, right?"

I shook my head and crossed my arms over my chest. "Don't you say it, Logan Birch."

"You know I'm right, babe."

I stabbed my finger into his chest. "Do not go there."

Lo stepped closer and placed one hand on my waist. "I don't know why you let it happen."

I growled low.

"It happens every time. It's like you think it's going to end differently, but it never does."

"Papa Lo, you made Mama Meg growl!" Jonas let out a peel of laughter that penetrated my pissed mood.

A smile cracked my down-turned lips. "I'm smiling at Jonas, not you," I clarified.

Lo hitched his thumb over his shoulder. "He is pretty damn cute. I should have sent him here."

"You are not allowed to use the kid in our arguments. That is a rule." Totally not fair.

Lo placed his other hand on my waist and pulled me into his arms. "I don't think I've ever seen you this hangry before."

"I hate that you know me so well."

Lo shrugged. "Been with you for over ten years, babe. I should know you."

The doorbell rang and my stomach let out a loud growl. "Thank freaking god." I let out a relieved sigh and headed to the front door with Jonas hot on my heels.

I yanked open the door and came face to face with Larry.

Oh no. This was not the time to deal with Larry when I was in the middle of a hangry bout.

Not. Good. At. All.

"Papa Lo!" Jonas called.

See, even Jonas knew that this was not going to end well.

"Oh fuck," Lo muttered.

"Papa Lo!" Jonas hollered again. "You can't say that."

"Yup, sorry about that, buddy." Lo came up behind me and gently moved me off to the side of the door

"Logan. Nice to see you."

I rolled my eyes at Larry's words and grabbed Jonas's hand. I tugged him toward the couch to wait for the pizza with me and listen to whatever Larry had to say.

"I've found more poop on my lawn."

Lo didn't even have a chance to say hello before Larry started in on the poop on his lawn. If I stayed hangry there was a good chance I would go take a huge deuce in the middle of his lawn if he kept it up.

Lord, I was really hangry.

"I told you, Larry, we don't have a dog anymore. Blue passed away a few months ago."

"I miss Blue," Jonas announced.

I put my arm around his shoulder and pulled him close. "Me too, Buddy. He was the best puppy." Now I am going to poop on Larry's lawn for coming over to bring up Blue again and making Jonas and I sad.

"I know, I know," Larry repeated. "But I think I know what it is that is pooping on my lawn." Larry pulled out a digital camera and held it up to Lo's face.

"It's a dog, Larry."

Jonas giggled and even I had to laugh at Lo's deadpan tone.

"But it's not anyone's dog, Lo. He's a stray," Larry stressed.

"Then call the humane society or something. I don't know what to tell you, Larry."

"Wait." I jumped up from the couch and pushed Lo to the side to see the camera Larry was still holding up. "He's just a puppy," I gushed. He was mostly black with a white chest and brown by his eyes and ears.

"I know. I tried to catch him but he was too quick for me." Larry sighed. "I don't know why the little crapper thinks he needs to poop on my lawn."

Maybe because Larry referred to him as a crapper. Seem like good karma working to me.

"What are you going to do when you catch him?" I asked.

Larry shrugged. "Probably take him to the pound."

Probably? Yeah, I didn't like the sound of that. "We'll catch him."

"We will?" Jonas and Lo said in unison. Except Jonas sounded excited and Lo did not sound thrilled at all.

I pulled out my phone and took a picture of the puppy on the camera. "Yup. We sure will. Don't worry about the dog, Larry. We've got it under control." I closed the door in his face and turned the lock.

"What the hell just happened?" Lo asked.

I smiled widely. "We just figure out the one thing that can cure me being hangry if I don't have food."

"A stray dog?" Lo asked.

"More like catching a puppy."

Life was hectic having Jonas with us now, but what would it hurt to add an adorable puppy to the mix?

*

Lo

"Babe."

"Shh, Lo. You're going to scare him away."

I rolled my eyes. "Pretty sure you crunching on those chips like a man starving is what is going to scare him away."

She popped another chip in her mouth and held the binoculars up to her eyes. "We should have gotten those where we could see in the dark."

"I was not going to spend that much money on a pair of binoculars that we were going to use one time." After Larry had come over to let us know about the stray puppy, Meg was a man on a mission bound and determined to rescue the puppy and make it hers. When the pizza finally got delivered Meg grabbed the two boxes, me and Jonas, and loaded us all in the truck to go shopping for puppy rescue supplies.

I didn't know exactly what puppy rescue supplies were until we were checking out at the pet store with a cart full of treats, toys, a pet bed, and a pair of binoculars meant for bird watching. Meg was crazy as hell, but she had a heart bigger than anyone I had ever met

She knew absolutely nothing about this puppy other than a blurry picture Larry had taken, but she was going to catch him and make him our new family pet.

"But how am I supposed to see Brutus when he walks onto Larry's yard to take a poop?" she whined.

"Larry took the picture around two AM yesterday. We got another hour until he might show up."

Meg snuggled under her blanket and put her feet up in my lap. "Is it supposed to get cold tonight?"

I rubbed her feet and relaxed back in my chair. "If I say yes does that mean we can sleep in our bed tonight and not the lawn chairs on the deck?"

Meg shook her head. "No. I just need to know if I should go in to get another blanket and the hand warmers."

"Babe, you really think you're ready for a new dog?" Meg had Blue for seventeen years and she was destroyed when she woke up to see he had passed away in his sleep.

She shrugged and tossed her arm over her head. "I think I'll know when I'm ready."

"You didn't answer the question," I chuckled.

"Lo," she mumbled. "I'll know if I want this puppy. Right now I know I need to help him so he isn't living on the street and pooping on Larry's yard. God knows what Larry would do to him if he caught him."

"So what if you don't want him but Jonas does?"

Meg waved her hand at me. "You're worrying about something that hasn't happened yet. For all we know the puppy won't come around and you're sitting here worrying about nothing." She sighed softly. "Will tell you one thing though."

"What's that, babe?"

"If I jive with this puppy, and he wants to live with us, you can bet your ass he's going to poop on Larry's yard every morning."

*

Chapter Twenty-Four

Meg

"Lo, stop." I batted away Lo's hand and tried to roll over.

Big mistake.

I instantly remembered I was sleeping in a lawn chair and froze. My arms wrapped around what I thought was Lo's arm, but it wiggled against me.

"Oh, my god!" I whispered.

Lo and I had passed out sometime after two and I had been hopeless that the puppy was going to show up.

I was wrong.

The black little fellow was curled up in my arms with his nose buried in my blanket.

"Lo," I whisper shouted. "Wake up."

Lo stirred but didn't wake up.

"Oh my gosh," I gasped when the little puppy opened his eyes and looked up at me.

I knew right then and there.

This was going to be my puppy.

He was pretty dirty, but he seemed to be eating well and he obviously wasn't afraid of people.

"Lo," I called again.

This time he cracked open one eye and looked at me. "You got a dog," he stated obviously.

"Thank god you woke up to tell me that," I scoffed. I scratched the top of the little puppy's head and he closed his eyes blissfully. "He climbed into my arms when I was sleeping, Lo. He felt safe with me."

"I know that look," he grumbled. "You already decided that ball of fur is yours, didn't you?"

I adjust the little guy in my arms and looked him in the eye. "I'm pretty sure he chose me, Lo. I can't turn him away."

Lo dropped his feet to ground and scooted to the edge of the chair. He reached over to pet the puppy and scratched him behind the ear. "You know what he is?"

"A dog, Lo."

Lo rolled his eyes. "I mean, is he really a boy or a girl?"

"Oh, sorry. My sarcasm is apparently strong today."

"That's every day," Lo grumbled.

I lifted the puppy up to see if he was packing equipment or not. "Frank and beans," I laughed. The little guy whined and tried to burrow back into my lap.

"What breed do you think he is?" Lo asked.

I really didn't know much about dogs other than I thought they were all adorable. "The breed that I'm going to keep."

Lo stood up and held his hand out to me. "Well, let's get inside. Our mission is accomplished."

"What time is it?" I asked. It was still dark out and it didn't seem like the sun was going to rise anytime soon.

"Three-thirty. We can get a couple hours of sleep before Jonas wakes up if we're lucky."

I slowly rose from the chair and cradled the puppy in my arms. "You ever get the feeling that everything is right? Like this is exactly where you should be?"

Lo opened the front door and held it for me. "Every morning when I wake up next to you, babe."

"Aw," I sighed. I nestled the puppy's nose to mine. "You have the sweetest daddy ever now. He may seem all rough and tough, but he's actually pretty damn sweet."

"Don't tell him all of my secrets." Lo closed the door behind us and slid the lock into place. "Do I even have to ask where he is sleeping?"

I grabbed the puppy bed off the floor and headed into the bedroom. "He needs a bath, but I'm going to put his bed on our bed and have him sleep in there."

Of course. I wasn't surprised at all that Meg was going to put a stray dog in our bed after having him for about five minutes. "You think he's actually going to sleep?"

She shrugged and placed the dog bed in the middle of our big bed. "Guess it's a good thing you broke that big ass bed all of those years ago."

Meg wrinkled her nose at me and placed the puppy in the bed. "He can also be a butt, puppy. You just gotta remember he has that sweet in there."

"We gonna give him a name or just keep calling him puppy?" I flipped off the bedroom light and pulled back the covers on my side.

"I think we should let Jonas decide the puppy's name. I bet he would get a kick out of that."

"Speaking of Jonas." I headed out of the bedroom and into his room. He was again just sprawled out all over the bed with his mouth hanging open. The kid really relaxed when he slept.

"He's okay?" Meg asked when I walked back into the room.

I nodded my head and flipped off the lights. "Totally passed out. Sawing a few logs too." I climbed into bed and laid on my side to look at the puppy. He was curled up on the dog bed and already back asleep. "He seems pretty young, doesn't he?"

Meg nodded her head. "Yeah, he really is. We'll have to get him to the vet right away on Monday. Today we'll just give him a bath and look him over."

I scratched the top of his and he gave a little whine. "He's a cutie."

Meg smothered a yawn with the back of her hand. "He sure is. In the morning we'll try to get a better look at him to figure out what he is." Meg laid her head down on her pillow but kept her hand on the puppy.

"That's how you're going to sleep, isn't it?"

She nodded her head and closed her eyes. "Yup. If he moves to go potty or try to jump down, I'll wake up. I did the same thing with Blue when he was a baby."

"Is he your new Blue, babe?"

Meg shook her head. "No. I'll never have another Blue, but maybe I'll have another amazing puppy."

I sure hoped so. As soon as Jonas woke up and saw him, there was going to be no turning back on keeping the little guy.

*

Chapter Twenty-Five

Meg

"Red."

"Really?" I asked.

Jonas nodded his head.

"But he doesn't have any red on him." I cuddled the puppy to my chest. "What about Rover or Bud?"

Jonas shook his head. "Nope. His name is Red. You had Blue, so now you need a Red."

The door to the exam room opened, and the vet walked in. "Meg," he called. "It's so good to see you." He held his hand out to me. "I'm so sorry to hear about Blue. He was one of a kind."

I mustered up a smile and shook his hand. "Thank you. He lived a good and long life."

"And now it's time for the next generation, right?" Dr. Thoms smiled at the puppy in my arms. "I don't have a name on my chart though. Are you still undecided?"

I glanced at Jonas and he smiled brightly. "Tell him, buddy."

"His name is Red. Mama Meg had Blue, so he needs to be Red."

"Well," Dr. Thoms laughed. "I really can't argue with that logic." He reached for Red and held him in his arms. "He sure is a cutie. Tell me what you can about him."

Dr. Thoms set him on the exam table and raised it up till Red was at chest height. A nurse came in and held Red in place while the Dr. looked him over.

"Uh, well, we've had him for about a day. Our neighbor had mentioned that there was a puppy wandering around, and it just felt right to rescue the little guy."

Dr. Thoms nodded his head. "Well, I can't help but like that story." He looked at his teeth and the puppy tried to lick him like he was a piece of steak. "From his size and teeth, I would say he is about ten weeks and a cross between a border collie and a Pitbull. He should be one smart puppy when he grows up."

The doctor finished his exam of Red and gave him the thumbs up that he was going to be okay. "Maybe feed him half a cup of food four times a day. He needs to gain a little weight, but other than that, he is absolutely perfect."

After the doctor gave the puppy a treat and Jonas a lollipop we were out of the vet's and headed back home.

"Mama Meg," Jonas called from the back seat.

"Yeah, buddy."

"Can we stop and get ice cream?"

I glanced in the rearview mirror. "Were you good in school today?"

Jonas shrugged. "I think so. Teacher didn't have to tell me to stop talking today."

Jonas couldn't say his teacher's name so he had just resorted to calling her teacher. Lo and I were picking up on it too. "Well, has Teacher told you that before?"

Jonas nodded his head. "Yes, but only when I talk a lot."

Oh, the logic of a four-year-old. "Then I guess we can stop and get an ice cream cone."

"Yay! Can we get one for Papa Lo?"

I laughed and nodded my head. "I guess if you think he's been good too."

"I do," Jonas exclaimed. "Red had been a good boy too! We should get him ice cream."

I turned into the parking lot of the ice cream place and pulled into the drive thru. "Maybe next time Red can get one, okay?"

Jonas stroked Red's head. "Sorry, Red, I tried."

Jonas and Red were quite the pair. They had only been together for a day, but they were already becoming the best of buds.

I handed Jonas's ice cream cone back to him, set Lo's dish of ice cream in the cupholder and held mine as I pulled back onto the road.

Not even a minute later Jonas was giggling in the backseat as Red jumped up on him and tried to steal his cone. Jonas held it out to him so he could lick it, then he took a lick for himself. It was so stinking cute that I didn't have the heart to tell him to stop.

Red was probably going to have the runs the next day or two, but it was worth it to see Jonas so happy and giggly.

*

Chapter Twenty-Six

Lo

"I gotta go, babe."

Meg lifted her head and looked at me confused. "Go where? It's almost eight o'clock."

"Got some club business to take care of."

She eyes me carefully. "Is this the same club business you talked about the first day of school?"

I nodded my head and shrugged on my cut. "Yeah."

"I don't like this club business, Lo. You should let someone else handle it."

I grabbed the keys to my motorcycle and shook my head. "Nah, that's not going to happen, babe."

She pursed her lips and glanced at Jonas who was sitting on the floor playing with his cars and trucks. "You have two more reasons to come home now, Lo. Are you sure this is worth possibly losing that?" She nodded to Jonas and Red.

"This is nothing, Meg. If it was dangerous, you know I wouldn't even think about going."

She rose from the couch and walked straight into my arms. "This is one of the reasons why I love you, Lo. You doing things like this to make sure it doesn't happen to anyone else." She tipped her head back. "You're not going to like, uh," she drug her finger across her neck, "eek?"

I laughed and grabbed her finger. I pressed a finger to the pad and smiled. "Just letting him know the proper way to treat a human being, babe."

She sighed and dropped her chin to her chest. She leaned into me and her head hit my shoulder. "Such a good man," she mumbled. "I guess I'll tell you the same thing I always do when you take off on club business." She wrapped her arms right around me and sighed. "Be careful and come home to me."

I pressed a kiss to the top of her head and squeezed her tight. "I always will, babe."

I ruffled Jonas's hair as I walked past and Red raised his head for a scratch. "Be good for Mama Meg, bud."

"Okay," he sang out.

Meg insisted on one more kiss and then she finally let me out of the house.

I threw my leg over my bike and cranked it up. The engine vibrated underneath me, and I kicked the kickstand up.

Today Demon and Gambler had given me all the info they had gotten the past few days on the principal and they both felt tonight was the night to make our move.

Once we took care of this asshole, things were going to go back to normal. Well, the new normal that included Jonas and Red.

The new normal that I wouldn't give up for anything.

170

I pulled up to the principal's house and saw the rest of the guys were already there.

"You're late," Rigid snickered.

I flipped him off and slid off the bike. "Doing the family thing, brother. Hard to pull me away from that."

Rigid nodded his head. "I hear that. We take care of this asshole and then we can all get back home."

Now that sounded like a damn good plan.

Demon, Rigid, and Slider followed me up the driveway to the front door and stood behind me when I knocked. "I'm assuming the rest of the guys are around back?" I asked before the door opened.

"That and somewhere else," Demon snickered.

The door opened before I could ask him what he meant by that.

Troy opened the door and swept his arm out. "Welcome, boys. So nice of you to join us."

I glanced back at Rigid. "I didn't know he was part of the plan."

Rigid shrugged. "He's got kids at the school, brother. Figured he had as much interest in this as we did."

He had a point but it would have been nice to have been clued in on him being here. I walked past Troy and into the large living room.

"Mr. Seth is awaiting you in the dining room," Troy called with a British accent.

"Never a dull moment when we're all together," Slider laughed.

We walked into the dining room and I couldn't help but laugh. George, the principal was sitting at the head of the long, rectangular table, his arms and legs tied, while Gambler and Gravel sat on each side of him while shoveling pot pie into their faces.

"Did I miss dinner?" I asked.

"We almost did, too," Gambler laughed. "Good ol' George here as kind enough to share with us."

"What do you want from me?" George shouted. "I said I was sorry about before."

I shook my head and pulled out the chair in front of me. "Sometimes saying sorry just isn't enough, Georgie."

Rigid, Demon, and Slider each found a chair and sat down around the table.

I pulled an envelope out of my pocket and laid it on the table.

"I really don't understand what you are doing here. My wife is going to be home any minute with my kids. You're going to scare them."

I laughed flatly. "Pretty sure you are the one who scares your wife, George, not me."

George's eyes darted around the room. "You don't know about my wife. You don't know anything about me."

172

I opened the envelope and laid out six pictures, face down. "You know when you grabbed my ass at school, George?"

His jaw dropped, and he looked embarrassed. "I don't know what you are talking about?"

"Oh, come on, Georgie, don't be embarrassed. We all know you enjoy some sausage now and then. There isn't anything wrong with that as long as the sausage you're wanting wants the same thing." I flipped open the first picture. "You really do have a pretty wife, George. If you're not going to treat her well, you should let her go so she could make someone else happy."

"How did you get that picture of her?" George demanded.

I nodded to Demon and Slider. "Oh, you didn't realize for the past few days you've had some company?"

Demon shook his head. "I couldn't have been more obvious, but you are so self fucking involved that you didn't even notice me."

I tsked and laid the picture of George's wife down on the table. I picked up the next picture and held it up.

"You better not have touched my children you sick assholes!" George roared.

I shook my head. "That's not my thing, George." I looked at the picture of the pretty girl who looked to be about thirteen. "That would be pretty awful of me to force myself onto someone like her though, wouldn't it?"

"No," George screamed. "Don't touch my children."

I set down the photo and picked up the next. "What is his name?" I asked as I held it up.

"You guys are sick fucking assholes! Let me go! You're not going to touch my children." George was in a rage over something that wasn't going to happen, but did it hurt to make him think that it might? After all, he constantly prayed on people who didn't want him touching them, but he still did it.

"Oh, now this one looks to be about my boys age." I held up the next photo. "Maybe just a little older than him."

George growled and tried to rip his arms out of the restraints. "Stop. Just stop," he insisted.

"It's pretty unsettling to sit here and think that someone could be forcing themselves on your wife and children, right, George?" I nodded to Rigid who stood up. He pulled a knife from his pocket and moved toward George.

"No, no," George pleaded. "Please don't do this. I promise I'll never touch anyone again." He shook his head fiercely back and forth. "Just leave my family alone."

Rigid pressed the knife to George's throat and sneered at him. "Make one wrong move and it's over for you, Georgie."

"I know it might seem crazy, but we're really not here to hurt you, George." I looked around the room. "We're more so here to help you see the light."

"Like angels," Gravel laughed.

"Angels of mercy," Demon elaborated.

"This is what is going to happen, George." I gathered all of the photos and tossed them at George. "You're gonna stop being a fucking douche canoe, and we're going to let you live."

"Thank you, thank yo-," George shouted

I held my hand up and cut him off. "There's a catch, Georgie. We're gonna be watching you, making sure that you walk a straight line. You so much as look at anyone who isn't your wife, and we'll cut your dick off and mail it to your mother." I pulled a small piece of paper out of my pocket. "1749 West Moreland Ave. Is that her address?"

"Yes, yes," George shouted. "Just please don't touch my mother. Please don't."

I rolled my eyes. "You really don't understand just what the Devil's Knights are about, do you, George?" I pointed to the pictures scattered around. "I'm not interested in hurting your family. They haven't done anything to deserve that. Hurting innocent people is not the type of business the Devil's Knights are in."

"But that seems to be what you're into though." Rigid moved the knife from George's throat and place the tip right over George's heart. "If you do it, why can't someone do it to your family?"

"I'm sorry, I'm sorry," George yelled. "I... I... I never thought about it like that. I didn't think!"

"No fucking shit," Gravel growled. "All you thought about was getting your dick wet. Didn't matter who or where it was."

"This is your last chance, George." I stood up and grabbed a picture off the table. "You take one step out of line, and I'll make sure you and your family never see the light of day again." I tucked the picture back into my pocket. "I'll be keeping this one for safekeeping." I walked out of the dining room and headed straight to my bike. I didn't want to be around that piece of shit anymore.

The Devil's Knights would never hurt his family, but he wasn't going to ever know that. As long as George walked the line, his life would be peachy.

If one toe went out of line though, you could bet your ass George would never see the light of day again.

*

Meg

"Lo?"

The bed shifted next to me, and a warm arm draped over my waist. "Just me, babe."

I rolled into him and laid my head on his shoulder. "You came home to me," I whispered. I never really thought he wouldn't if he had a choice, but I also knew tomorrow was never promised.

"Nothing can keep me away from you."

I hummed blissfully and relaxed into him.

"Where's Red?" he asked softly.

Red had slept in bed with us since we had gotten him, but Jonas had asked to let him sleep in his room tonight. I had given in, fully expecting to have to scoop both of them up and put them in bed with Lo and I. "He's sleeping with Jonas."

"So that means I get you and my bed all to myself?"

"For the time being," I whispered.

"Hell yeah," he growled.

I tipped my head back and looked Lo in the eye. "Is everything okay?"

He brushed his fingers down my cheek. "You asking about club business, babe?"

I rolled my eyes. "We've been married for ten years, Lo. You should know by now that whether you tell me or one of the girls does, that I always find out about club business." So foolish for him to think that he could keep it from me and that I wouldn't ask questions.

"We took care of him, Meg."

"What do you mean you took care of it?" I know Lo had said that they didn't plan to hurt Mr. Seth, but living around the club had taught me one thing, it was I knew sometimes things didn't always go to plan.

"I mean Mr. Seth is very much alive, but he has a completely new view on how to treat other human beings."

"And his family?"

Lo sighed. "His family wasn't anywhere around, Meg. Demon had a connection at the radio station. The wife and kids were at the movies after winning passes and concessions for six. They aren't going to know anything happened tonight."

I tried my fingers down his chest. "You really are a good man, Lo."

"Papa Lo?"

Lo closed his eyes and I could tell he was counting.

"Uh, hey, bud." I raised up on my elbow and saw Jonas and Red were at the end of the bed. "What are you two doing up?"

Jonas's voice sounded tired, and he rubbed the sleep from his eye with the back of his hand. "I think Red has to go to the bathroom and so do I."

Lo tossed the covers back. "I'll get Red, you get Jonas back in bed."

"Just remember you love this life," I called to Lo.

"Living the dream, babe," he hollered back.

I helped Jonas to the bathroom and listened to Lo tell Red he was a good boy while he hooked the harness on him.

It may be after midnight and Lo and I might not be able to spend the rest of the night the way we wanted, but I couldn't help but feel that we really were living the dream.

*

Chapter Twenty-Seven

Lo

"I gotta run to the store, but Jonas doesn't want to come." Meg stood in the doorway of my office at the clubhouse with her purse hitched over her shoulder. "Can he stay here with you?"

I nodded my head. "You know he can always come here, babe."

"I know, I know," she muttered. "You're just supposed to be working and I don't want to have him get in the way."

"Pretty sure you're the one who said you know what my work schedule is because you take all of the orders." I nodded toward the body shop. "Guys are busy, but I've got nothing going on today."

"Great. I didn't want to have to tell Jonas he had to come shopping with me."

I stood up and Meg moved to me. I wrapped my arms around her waist and she tipped her head back to look up at me. "You're looking good today, babe."

She rolled her eyes. "What are you buttering me up for?" she laughed.

I shook my head. "I can't appreciate how good my wife looks?"

"You can, but not when we're in your office and Jonas is six feet away."

My hand squeezed her ass, and I pulled her close. "Then I guess tonight I'm continuing my appreciation after the boy goes to sleep."

She tapped a finger to my lips. "Good thinking, honey."

"You bring Red with you?"

She nodded her head. "You know Red and Jonas are attached to each other. We've only had Red for three weeks, but they're bound to be buddies for life."

"Just like you wanted."

Meg pouted out her bottom lip. "I actually wanted him to be my buddy for life, but you know, I need to be the adult and not demand Red be my dog."

I pressed a kiss to her lips. "Then maybe you need to get another dog?"

Her eyes lit up and her jaw dropped. "Don't say that to me, Logan Birch. You know how I am with puppies."

"Wouldn't say it if I didn't mean it."

She snaked her arms around my neck and laid a hell of a kiss on me. "You just fully slipped me into the Lo Daze."

I shrugged. "What can I say? I've got the touch."

"And puppies," she laughed.

Meg breezed out of the office with a spring in her step and a new puppy on her mind.

I went in search of Jonas and found him sitting on his dad's bike in the shop. Rigid was with him, pointing out all the upgrades on it.

After the accident the shop had been to pick up Turtle's bike, and we had been working on rebuilding it since. There were still a few things that needed to be done with it, but she was mostly complete.

"Hey, bud."

"Papa Lo," Jonas shouted. "Come look at my dad's bike!"

Rigid kept his hand on Jonas until I made my way over to the bike. He nodded to me and headed back into the shop.

"You like it?" he asked me. He gripped the handlebars and beamed up at me. "I wanna go for a ride on it."

"Oh yeah?"

He nodded his head. "Yes. Can we go now?"

I shook my head. "Not quite yet. But as soon as it's done you and I will take it out."

Jonas blew out a raspberry and pretended to drive the bike.

"You know this is yours right, bud?"

He looked up at me, shocked. "It is?"

I nodded my head. "It is. Your dad was one of my best friends and I know for a fact that if anyone would have his bike, that it would be you."

Jonas nodded his head. "I miss him sometimes."

I lifted Jonas from the bike and held him in my arms. "That's okay, buddy. He was your dad. He loved you more than anything."

"But sometimes I forget stuff."

I sat down sideways on the bike with Jonas in my lap. "What kind of stuff do you forget?"

"I don't know. I guess I just forget that I miss him."

I ruffled his hair and laughed. "I don't know if that makes sense, buddy."

Jonas sighed. "I just... sometimes I forget about him and mama."

Oh. "Listen, bud." I turned him in my lap and looked down at him. "You'll never forget your mom and dad. They're always going to be in your heart and mind."

"But... I have fun with you and Mama Meg."

"That's a good thing. That is what your mom and dad wanted when they said they wanted you to live with us if they couldn't be here anymore." I sighed and tried to think how to explain what Jonas was feeling. "How about this, bud? Your dad was my best friend. We were pretty alike. I think that's why he wanted me and Meg to take care of you. He knew I would be the closest replacement to him so you won't ever forget him."

"Daddy wants me to like you and Meg?"

I couldn't help but laugh. This was definitely going to have to be a conversation that we revisited at a later time. "He wants you to love us because we love you, Jonas. We don't want to replace your mom and dad, but we want you to know that we're going to be there for you just like they were there for you."

Jonas looked at the handlebars. "I want to be just like my dad when I grow up."

"Then that is exactly what you're going to do." I hugged Jonas tight. "I'm gonna be here every step of you becoming your dad, Jonas. From learning to ride a bicycle and driving this motorcycle for the first time. Hell, we're gonna need new prospects for the club eventually too."

"Just like dad," Jonas whispered.

Some things Jonas didn't quite get, but when it came to his dad, he knew just what he was. "Second generation, bud. You and the rest of the kids are the future of the club." I had never really thought about it before, but all those kids were the future of the club.

Only God knew what was going to happen down the road, but I knew the Devil's Knights weren't going anywhere as long as we kept the brotherhood and the traditions of the club alive.

Long live the Devil's Knights.

The End

This is the end of the road for the first generation of the
Devil's Knights.
Lo, Rigid, and the rest of the club made the Knights what
they are today.
Will the next generation bask and grow in the brotherhood,
or will they buck tradition and forge their own path?

Devil's Knights, 2nd Generation

Passing the Torch
May 29th, 2020

Coming Soon

Brinks
Fallen Lords MC, Book 9

January 29th

About the Author

Winter Travers is a devoted wife, mother, and aunt turned author who was born and raised in Wisconsin. After a brief stint in South Carolina following her heart to chase the man who is now her hubby, they retreated back up North to the changing seasons, and to the place they now call home.

Winter spends her days writing happily ever after's, and her nights with her hubby and son. She also has an addiction to anything MC related, her dog Thunder, and Mexican food! (Tamales!)

Winter loves to stay connected with her readers. Don't hesitate to reach out and contact her.

Facebook: www.facebook.com/wintertravers
Twitter: https://twitter.com/wintertravers
Instagram: https://www.instagram.com/wintertravers/
Website: www.wintertravers.com
Mailing List: http://eepurl.com/bYpIrD
Goodreads: https://bit.ly/2vAJPm1
BookBub: https://bit.ly/2HQtk7y

Dive into the first chapter of **Drop a Gear and Disappear**!

Drop a Gear and Disappear

Kings of Vengeance MC

Book 1

Chapter One

Quinn

A lady in the streets and a freak in the bed…

"Come with me, baby."

Kimber rolled into my side. "I'll pass."

I looked down at her naked body and ran my fingers over her smooth, flawless skin. "You're gonna have to come there one day."

"But today is not that day, Quinn."

"It's Gear, baby."

She snorted and tipped her head back to look at me. "Okay, Quinn."

I fucking hated my name, yet Kimber insisted on calling me it even though I finally got my road name from the

Rolling Devils. "You gotta learn to tolerate the club, baby. I know you don't like it, but you gotta not hate it."

"Mmhmm," she hummed under her breath and laid her head back on my shoulder. Her hand slid across the expanse of my chest, and her fingers trailed over the tattoo of an eagle holding a skull. "But you don't need to leave just yet," she whispered.

"Soon."

"Maybe I need to remind you what will be waiting for you while you're fetching beers for all of your club buddies."

"I do more than that."

"Right," she drawled.

At least on normal days, I did more than that. On nights like tonight, I did basically just fetch beer and booze the whole time. "So what exactly are you going to do to make me not forget about you?"

She rolled onto her back and slowly raised her hands over her head. "It's more like what are you going to do."

I turned onto my side and slid my hand down between her tits. "Daddy's choice?" I whispered.

Her eyes flared with desire.

I was a lucky fucker to have Kimber in my bed.

The saying "a lady in the streets and a freak in the bed" was Kimber to a T.

During the day, she worked at a doctor's office where she answered phones and dealt with bitchy ass people with a smile on her lips, and at night, she was my naughty little minx who couldn't get enough of me.

I grabbed her by the waist and flipped her over onto her stomach. "On your knees, ass in the air."

She scampered up to her knees and wiggled her ass at me. I moved behind her, my knees between her legs, and slapped her ass. "Always hungry for my cock," I growled.

She looked over her shoulder at me with her bottom lip between her teeth and nodded her head. "Always," she whispered.

My hand wrapped around my cock, and I stroked up and down with my eyes never leaving hers. "Greedy pussy."

She reared back and bumped her ass against my hand. "Stop talking and start doing."

I gripped the globe of her ass and parted her cheeks. Her pussy was dripping, and the bud of her ass begged to be fucked. "Anything I want, baby?"

"I guess that all depends on what time you need to leave," she replied coyly.

I knew I didn't have the time to fuck her properly. She was trying to distract me from going to the club, but I couldn't miss the party. I pressed my dick against the entrance to her

192

pussy and slowly pushed in. "Your ass is mine later tonight," I promised.

She reared back again, her ass grinding against me. "Promises, promises," she muttered.

Damn right, it was a fucking promise. It was one I planned on keeping, too. I grabbed a handful of her hair and pulled her head back. "I'm gonna fuck you so hard, you aren't going to be able to get out of bed the whole time I'm gone."

"Yes," she hissed.

I put a hand on her hip and thrust deep. "Who do you belong to, Kimber?" I demanded.

"You," she breathed out.

"Say my name."

A sultry laugh fell from her lips. "Does one name get me a fucking and the other a spanking?"

"Damn straight, baby. Choose carefully."

She rubbed her ass against me and flexed the walls of her pussy around my dick. "As fun as a spanking sounds, I need your dick."

I slowly pulled out then slammed back into her. "Like that? You want it hard?"

She groaned and shook her head. "Yes, Daddy."

I let go of her hair and grabbed her hips.

She dropped her head to the mattress and braced her arms. "Please, Gear. Fuck me."

She spoke the words she knew would drive me crazy and give her exactly what she wanted.

With each thrust of my hips, she moaned my name.

My fingers dug into her hips as I held her still and drove into her. "Tell me again," I grunted.

"I'm yours," she gasped. "I'm yours, Gear."

I felt her climax climbing and moved faster. "Play with yourself, baby." I was going to come soon, and I wanted her pussy to milk every last drop of cum from me.

Her hand snaked between her legs. "Gear, please," she pleaded. "Fuck me."

While her fingers stroked her clit, my dick pounded her pussy.

"I'm...I'm coming," she whimpered. "Gear...please."

Her pussy contracted around my dick as her orgasm washed over her, and she ripped my release from me. "Fuck yeah," I grunted. "Take it all, baby."

She panted my name then buried her face in the pillow.

The final tremors rocked through me, and I fell onto the mattress next to her.

She dropped the rest of the way and partially rolled into me.

I threw an arm over her and pulled her close. "Sure you don't want to come with me?" I asked again. "We could find a room at the clubhouse and find the time to do that all over again."

She laughed and shook her head. "Or I could just stay here, eat some pizza, and sleep until you get home."

"It's gonna be late." I didn't expect to leave the clubhouse 'til well into the morning.

"Just wake me up when you get home."

She wasn't going to budge on this. I had been a prospect for the club four months, and she refused to even step foot at the clubhouse. "One day, I'm going to get you to come to a party."

She scoffed. "But that day is not today," she laughed.

I pressed a kiss to the side of her head and rolled out of bed. She pulled the blanket over her body and turned onto her back. "You didn't need to cover up."

She rolled her eyes and fluffed the pillow under her head. "Last I checked, if you're not in this bed, then you don't have a say about what I'm wearing or doing."

I grabbed the blanket and tugged it down her body 'til I could see her tits. "Is that so?"

She grabbed the blanket to tug it up, but I didn't let it go. "You're gonna be late, Quinn," she tried to reason.

"I'm already late, Kimber. My ass should have been on my bike half an hour ago, but your greedy pussy kept me in bed."

She scooted down the bed and managed to get under the covers enough to conceal her body from me. "Well, this pussy is staying in bed cause I had a long day at work and since you just fucked me twice, I think a nap is needed before I order pizza."

"A nap and pizza, huh?" That did seem like a good night, but the club couldn't be put off. I let go of the blanket and bent to pick up my clothes. "Save me a slice, and don't put fucking olives on it."

She snuggled under the blanket and watched me get dressed. "How many people are going to be there tonight?"

This was the fourth large party the club had since I had started prospecting, and each one kept getting bigger than the last. "I think a shit-ton. I don't get to sit in on the meetings, but Mud had mentioned another club was coming in for the night."

"Still can't believe the guy who is your sponsor goes by the name Mud."

I shrugged on my shirt. "Baby, I told you road names can be anything. You should be happy and realize I was lucky to get a name like Gear and not Mud or Bug." I pulled on my socks and then my pants.

She wrinkled her nose. "Doesn't mean I have to like it."

I sat down on the edge of the mattress and pulled on my shoes. "But you don't have to bust my balls about it all of the time," I reminded her.

"I know," she sighed. "I promise I'll come to the next party with you. I just don't want to go to one of these and then be left all alone because you have some obligation to grab someone a beer every five minutes."

I stood up and turned to look down at her. "You're really going to go to the next one?" I asked, surprised. I really didn't think I was ever going to be able to get her to come to the clubhouse.

She nodded. "Only for you, though. I'm not interested in making friends with the other chicks."

"They're called ol' ladies, Kimber," I chuckled. "And I happen to know when the next party is."

"Oh God," she laughed. "I have time to look forward to dreading going."

I shook my head. "You won't have to wait long. Tomorrow night is another party."

Her jaw dropped. "Wait...what?" she squawked. "I can't...you didn't..."

She knew there wasn't a way in hell that I was going to let her go back on her promise of coming to the next party. I leaned down and pressed a kiss to her lips. "Get some rest, baby. You're going to need it for the party tomorrow."

I strutted out of the room and straight out of our apartment.

Kimber may not like the club, but she was going to start coming to these damn parties with me.

She had said she would, and I wasn't going to let her go back on her word.

*

Made in the USA
Middletown, DE
26 December 2019